CW01658671

THE DOUBLE

JOANNE RYAN

© Joanne Ryan 2022

Tamarillas Press

All Rights Reserved. No part of this publication may be reproduced or transmitted in any form or by any means, electronic or mechanical, including photocopy, recording, or any information storage and retrieval system, without permission from the author.

This book is a work of fiction. All characters, locations, businesses, organisations and situations in this publication are either a product of the author's imagination or used factiously. Any resemblance to real persons, living or dead, is purely coincidental.

Cover Design: © Joanne Ryan
ISBN: 978-1-913807-15-3

Other books by Joanne Ryan:
Without Reason
All The Lost Years
Not Your Average Girl
The Lodger
Lie To Me
One Night

Writing as Marina Johnson:
Fat Girl Slim
Fat Girl Slim Returns
Fat Girl Slim Three
A Confusion of Murders
Say Hello & Wave Goodbye
The Herb Sisters
The Harriet Way
So Talk To Me

CHAPTER ONE

I saw my double today.

Apparently, everyone has a double out there somewhere, but I never really believed it until today, because how would it even be possible? What are the chances of all of the different combinations of parents producing someone who is exactly the same as someone else who isn't even related to them? Impossible, I used to say.

Until now.

Right, so it *is* possible, but what are the chances of actually meeting your double? Non-existent, I would have said, or if I was a betting person, a billion-to-one chance. Because even if you have a double they could live in a different town, a different country or a different continent.

And yet, there I was, sitting opposite my very own doppelganger.

I was travelling on a train that I shouldn't have been on, going somewhere that I wouldn't normally have been going to and suddenly, there she was, sitting right in front of me.

She wasn't wearing a mask but I was, so she couldn't see that I was *her* double because the bottom of my face was covered. The pandemic may be over and life may be more or less back to normal but some of us are still hanging onto our masks. We've got used to them, we like them because we can hide behind them and somehow, they make you feel invisible. I always wear one, not because I'm afraid of catching any lingering Covid germs but because I like the anonymity. If ever I go to the shops or on public transport, I always put one on.

People don't bother to try and make small talk with you if you have a mask on, it's too much effort and the very fact that you're wearing a mask says *don't talk to me.* It also makes it easier to ignore people you know; keep your eyes forward and don't look at them and you can pretend you haven't seen them and your expression doesn't betray you because they can't see it. Of course, that's if you don't feel like talking to people, which I don't, mostly.

There are enough of us still wearing masks to make it appear normal and not freakish and I never go anywhere without taking one with me. I've noticed that it's mostly women who are still wearing them so maybe they think the same way as I do. Or maybe it's because you don't have to bother with any make-up if you wear a mask. My mum never leaves the house without a mask although she does have an ulterior motive; it's easier for her to fool the shop CCTV with half of her face covered when she's shoplifting.

Anyway, there I was this morning, sitting on the mid-morning train bound for London. I don't normally go into London; I live in a large town with plenty of shops and I can't afford to waste money on a train ticket just to window shop for stuff that I can't afford to buy. I was only on the train because I'd won a competition for a free re-style with a top London hairdresser. When I received the letter to tell me I'd won I honestly thought it was a wind-up because I couldn't even remember *entering* any competitions or prize draws. I rang the hairdressers to check and gave them the voucher number and yes, it was true, I could choose anything I liked, a colour, cut, anything. The train tickets were included and also a voucher for lunch at a nearby upmarket cafe.

I couldn't believe my luck and when I thought about it, I realised that Mum must have entered my details into a prize draw to maximise the chances of winning because she does it *all* the time. I don't think she thought it through properly because if she had, she'd know that if my name's on the ticket then I'm keeping the prize. Luckily for her it wasn't a car or something like that. Not that I was going to tell her that I'd won; no way, because she'd only demand that I give her the prize. I was delighted with the prize but thought it would have been a better prize if I could have taken someone with me but there was only one train ticket included and one voucher for lunch. I couldn't afford to fork out on another ticket for someone else to come along.

Although realistically, the only person I'd want to take with me would be Mac, and there's no way he'd set foot in a woman's hairdressers. *Have fun*, he'd said when he'd called me this morning, and then he'd lowered his voice and said he was looking forward to having a *new woman* in his bed tonight. My stomach flipped over in excitement when he said it because it meant he'd definitely be home when I got back. Mac never makes promises he doesn't keep.

So, there I was, minding my own business and enjoying having a good seat with a table to sit at and a window to look out of and Mac to dream of. I'd only been on the train for fifteen minutes when we pulled into the next station and a woman got on and sat herself down in the seat opposite me. Even though there was a table between us I was annoyed and I pulled a face at her underneath my mask and mouthed at her to *fuck off*, which is another good reason for wearing a mask. The carriage was only half-full and I couldn't understand why she had to sit at *my* table when she could have had another table all to herself. That's what I'd have done if it had been me, but maybe that's because I don't see the need to be surrounded by people all of the time like others do.

As soon as she'd settled into her seat, she put her mobile phone and her huge cup of *Costa* coffee on the table in front of her and leaned her head back against the headrest and closed her eyes. I thought it was a bit odd to be tired so early in the morning but it did give me a good chance to look at her.

The weird thing was that I didn't realise that she was my double straight away. I looked at her and thought that there was something very familiar about her. The thought crossed my mind that I knew her but I quickly dismissed that idea because I don't have very many friends and she definitely wasn't one of them. A celebrity, I mused, because she was very well-dressed with immaculate make-up and expensively styled hair.

It sounds laughable but it's true; I didn't immediately recognise my own double.

When it dawned on me that she looked exactly like me, I couldn't take my eyes off her; it was almost like looking in a mirror. It's a very strange feeling sitting opposite your double and looking at your own face on someone else. At one point I actually closed my eyes and opened them again to make sure that I wasn't seeing things or dreaming, or something.

She was oblivious to my scrutiny and even if she'd had her eyes open, she would have had no idea that she was sitting opposite her twin because my face was half-covered with a mask.

Her face was a perfect copy of mine.

Or mine was a perfect copy of hers.

Her hair was different though. Mine is, or was, dark brown and slightly wavy and hangs around my face not doing very much. I normally just scoop it up into a pony-tail. Her hair was near enough the same colour as mine but she had expensive-looking coppery low-lights running through it and it was super glossy and shiny. It was cut in that choppy S-wave hairstyle just below her chin that all the celebs seem to go for and looks really chic. I decided there and then that I was going to get my hair cut just like it at the swanky hairdressers I was going to.

Her clothes were very different to mine. I could tell from one glance that hers were much more expensive than my market knock-offs and Primark copies. Her pale-blue belted raincoat was the real *Stella McCartney* and not a fake; I could just *tell.* One of my main pastimes is reading all the celebrity magazines and I know pretty much every stitch on that coat because it's a personal favourite of mine. I know for a fact that it costs nearly nine-hundred-pounds yet she was wearing it with such casual confidence that it could have cost her a fiver. Only people with money have that disregard for the cost of things; her handbag lying on the seat next to her was a *Mulberry* and her mobile phone the very latest model, yet she'd tossed it onto the table as if it cost nothing.

Well off people are like that. I used to go with Mum and help her when she was a cleaner and all the big houses she cleaned were stuffed with expensive stuff that the rich owners just left lying around for anyone to steal. They didn't look after it like I would. Nothing bad had ever happened to them and those sort of people just assume that it never will. It drove Mum mad because there was all this expensive stuff just lying around and waiting to be taken and she couldn't nick any of it. They'd have known straight away that she'd taken it. She might be a thief but she's not stupid; she's been shoplifting for years and has managed to stay out of prison. She's been caught a few times but has always managed to get off with a fine. Although if they catch her again it might be different.

I felt a sudden surge of jealousy at my double's wealth and her disregard for it as I sat there. A small part of me wanted to reach my hand across the table and take hold of her fancy phone and slide it into my pocket.

I didn't, of course, because while my mother may be a common thief and shoplifter, I'm not.

Not for small stuff, anyway.

I noted her expensive clothes and designer handbag and I knew she'd have a very different life from mine even though our faces were exactly the same. She looked to be about the same size as me and her head was on a level with mine so I guessed we were around the same height, too.

After a while the ticket inspector arrived at our table and she couldn't really have been asleep because she opened her eyes and looked up at him. She smiled in that vague sort of way that well-off people do to everyone they meet and I was amazed to see that she even had the same teeth as me. The only words she spoke were *thank you* and just from those two words I could hear that her voice was similar to mine but her accent; well, let's just say she's what I could have been if I'd come from a rich family and gone to a private school.

So what do you do when you meet your double? Should I pull down my mask and say *ta-da!* Or take my mask off and wait for her to notice me? I was pondering this as she sat up and took a sip of her coffee. She glanced briefly at me and did that vague smile thing again and then leaned over her phone and opened up her *Instagram* page.

I didn't say a word or take my mask off because whilst I was marvelling at my mirror image sitting opposite me, it came to me.

She could be the answer to everything.

CHAPTER TWO

I can't help admiring myself in the darkness of the train window, my hair is super glossy and I keep moving my head slowly from side to side to watch it swing. If my double was on this train, she'd definitely notice me now, mask or no mask.

Alun, the stylist (with a U, he was at great pains to tell me, as if it mattered) seemed to know exactly what I wanted as soon as I started to speak. Although he did sniff as he held my hair up with his hands on each side of my head and let it drop. Each time he let my hair drop I felt as if I'd failed some sort of test but I have no idea what the test was. He did this several times with a snooty look on his face before ordering me over to the basin where a school-leaver with far too much makeup on washed my hair.

Quite honestly, I did feel out of place and awkward amongst all the well-off and glamorous women having their hair done in there. I very rarely go the hairdresser and when I do it's for a dry cut at *Savercuts* in the precinct. No one's well-off or snooty in there. My clothes felt cheap and the boots that I loved when I bought them from Primark felt plastic and nasty. Alun had a snotty look on his face and I had the feeling that he felt it was beneath him to do my hair because he made no conversation with me at all but was gushing with everyone else. It might have been free but I can't say it was an enjoyable experience.

He did do a good job though because my hair looked amazing by the time I left. When he'd finished there was no denying that I looked the absolute image of my double on the train.

After I came out of the hairdressers I trotted along to the cafe and slowly walked by so I could see what it was like. The windows were massive so I could see right in and the place was full of chunky oak tables with uncomfortable looking wooden chairs arranged on each side of them. Massive smoked glass lights that looked like giant light-bulbs hung down over the tables and they were all on even though it wasn't dark. There were quite a few people sitting in there having lunch or coffee and they were smartly dressed city types and quite a few were working on laptops. I knew that I would feel just as uncomfortable sitting in there as I did at the hairdressers so when I pushed the door open and went in, I'd already decided that I'd get a sandwich to takeaway.

As I stood at the counter waiting, I noticed that even the waitresses looked superior with their black wraparound aprons and messy up-dos. The baristas were even worse, snooty-looking, super-thin and more like runway models than someone who served drinks for a living. I selected a cheese and ham Panini, lemon meringue puff and a bottle of *Diet Coke* even though my voucher would have bought me a proper, hot meal if I'd sat inside. The cashier was at great pains to tell me that I wouldn't be able to have any change from the voucher but I didn't care. No way did I want to sit in that cafe and feel as uncomfortable as I did in the hairdressers.

I couldn't even find a bench or anywhere to sit to eat my sandwich when I came out so I had to take it with me to eat on the train. By the time I got to the station the return train carriage was heaving with passengers; luckily, I had a seat booked otherwise I would have had to travel the whole journey standing up. My doppelganger was nowhere to be seen but I already knew that she wouldn't be; she'd be staying at her home in London.

How did I know this?

Well, I had a good look on her *Instagram* profile where she was very free with information about herself. While she was sitting opposite me scrolling through *Instagram* on her phone, I made sure to memorise her name and any other information I could glean whilst reading her screen upside-down. I'm pretty good at reading upside-down and when I got off the train, I'd found her account before I'd even got to the hairdressers.

Once I'm settled in my seat, I open up my

sandwich and tuck in. For a snooty, expensive cafe it's a massive disappointment; dry and with barely any butter on it, I have to wash it down with mouthfuls of *Diet Coke*. I soon give in and put it back in the packet and start on the lemon puff but that isn't much better. When I've finished, I pull my phone out of my pocket and making sure that the man sitting next to me can't see, I scroll through her *Instagram* posts again and study them. The person in the photographs could be me; I could put my picture next to her and no-one would notice.

Katarina Hepworth-Jones.

I might have guessed she'd have a posh, double-barrelled name.

She has over a thousand followers but only follows two-hundred-and-fifty people herself. I can see from her posts that yesterday she spent the day catching up with an old friend and is now on her way home; hashtag *country life, old friends, catch ups, back to the smoke*. She's posted numerous pictures of her perfectly made-up face posing in front of pretty cottages, green fields, flowers and the front of the train station showing the name of the place. There aren't any photographs of the old friend, just a back view of a woman walking down a country lane with a dog, so maybe her friend didn't want to be on Instagram or Katarina just doesn't like to share the limelight.

I can't wait to show Mac her account and that I have a double – although my earlier feeling that somehow she's the answer to my prayers seems ridiculous now. How did I think that having a double who happens to be rich – and she is rich because her Instagram posts scream money – could benefit me in any way? Did I imagine that I could pretend to be her and people will just hand over money to me because I ask?

It's pathetic. I don't know what I thought, if I'm honest, and I feel embarrassed for even thinking that somehow, she could be the key to a new life for me.

I wish I had her life but I'd definitely want Mac to be in it. Katarina seems to spend most of her time having dinner at expensive restaurants, lounging around at spas and going on expensive holidays or visiting friends. And I don't think much of her husband; he looks old; much older than her. She's older than me by two years – twenty-eight to my twenty-six – but her husband looks a good twenty years older. He's a bit podgy and not even remotely good-looking but is obviously loaded because there's a glimpse of the front of a large house in some of her photos and others show an ultra-trendy back garden with lots of painted boards and a big summerhouse thing. There's also the nose of a flash looking sports car in several of the photos which I assume is his. I don't know anyone who lives in London but I do know that if you have a house with a garden, it costs a fortune.

I'm guessing she married him for his money

because it doesn't look as if she even has a job. Not that *I* have a job at the moment but that's different; I'm not living off a rich man, I'm living off the state. And I do work some of the time, just not at the moment. I'm having a well-deserved break before I start my next dead-end job.

I was considering going back into some sort of education to better myself because although I don't have many qualifications, I'm quite clever and quick on the uptake. Mum says I'm so sharp I'll cut myself one day but I'm not sure that she means it as a compliment. If it hadn't been so boring at school, I might have tried a bit harder instead of hanging out with my mates down the precinct. Although probably not, because being a swot was a death sentence socially and only for the students who absolutely didn't care if they went through their whole school life without one friend.

I'd even gone as far as getting some leaflets from the college to see what I might like to study for but that was before Mac and I got together. Mac's put me off the idea. Why go to college for years, Mac says, just to get a job that's going to pay barely more than the minimum wage?

He's got a point.

Nine to five isn't for him, he says, because he has no intention of wasting the best years of his life doing a shit job just so he can have a couple of weeks holiday a year and a bigger council house. Mac has plans; he says as soon as he's got enough money he's leaving this country and moving somewhere hot and sunny to live. My heart sank a bit when he said it because he said *I* and not *we*. I'm sure he meant me too because he wouldn't leave me behind, I'm sure he wouldn't. I know we haven't known each other for very long but we're good together; he's so different from any of the other men I've been out with. He's good looking, I mean *really* good looking, but it's not his looks, we *get* each other; we're on the same wave-length. Both of us feel that we're meant for better things but we just haven't figured out yet how we're going to get them.

And the chemistry, my God, when we're together we can't keep our hands off each other; *he* can't keep his hands off me. I feel a shiver go through me at the thought of him waiting for me when I get home; I've given him a key so he can let himself in to my flat anytime he likes. He has to work away a lot and I never know when he's coming back but I don't ever ask him because Mac *hates* needy women.

I remember how we met and I can't help thinking that he could easily meet someone better than me when he's working away but I have to put it out of my mind. I have to remind myself that he's with me and if I start getting jealous it'll drive him away and that'll be the end of us. Although it's hard not to torture myself with the thought of other women when he's away, especially at night when I'm alone in bed. But there's no need to fret over it now, because tonight he'll definitely be in *my* bed.

My phone bleeps and I close *Instagram* and open *Whatsapp* to see a message from Mac. He *knows* I'm thinking about him, *that's* how close we are; we're almost telepathic.

I'm home ☺

I smile, happy that he calls my place home.

Takeaway? he asks.

I start to reply but his next message beats me to it.

Before or after? His message asks, a winking emoji next it.

After. Definitely after. I type and press send.

I rest my head back against the headrest and close my eyes.

I think my new hair is going to get all messed up.

* * *

My hair got well messed up but such is the difference between a top London hairdresser and *Savercuts* on the precinct that I simply combed and shook it and it was as if I'd just walked out of the salon.

'Move aside, gorgeous, the food's arrived.' Mac comes into the lounge and sashays across the room, swinging his hips from side to side. He plonks several paper carrier bags on the coffee table with a flourish and flops onto the sofa next to me.

I laugh and look at him and marvel that even

the fact that he's wearing my pink dressing gown doesn't detract from his manliness. If anything, it enhances his masculinity.

'You need to get your own dressing gown,' I say.

'Nah,' he says, sitting down next to me. 'Dressing gowns are for old men. Anyway, if I'm wearing it, you can't, can you?' He leers at me theatrically and I try to pull his T-shirt that I'm wearing down enough to cover my legs.

'Don't,' he says, putting his hand on my thigh and stroking it. 'Why cover up such beautiful legs?'

I gaze at him and wonder how I got so lucky, he's not like the guys who live around here, as well as being gorgeous he isn't afraid to compliment me and talk about things other than football. I'm in love with him even though we've only known each other for a couple of months. I haven't told him this though, because he hasn't said it to me and I don't want to look *needy* and as if I expect some sort of commitment from him.

'Smells lush,' I say, changing the subject and sniffing the air. 'I'm starving.'

'Me too,' he says, taking his hand away and leaning over to the coffee table, he picks up the plates and hands me one.

We tuck into the Chicken Chow Mein with all the trimmings and in no time at all we're leaning back on the sofa, absolutely stuffed with food.

'Good Chinese,' Mac says, blowing out his cheeks. 'But I think I ate too much of it. Couldn't seem to stop myself once I started.'

'Nor me,' I agree. 'It was good, though.'

'We could always work it off,' Mac drawls, with a lazy wink.

'Maybe not yet,' I say, fearing that I'll vomit if I make any sort of sudden movement. 'And anyway, I've got something to show you.' I lean forward and pick up my phone and tap on the Instagram icon.

'Oh, not some social media crap, is it?' Mac says with a groan. 'You know I hate all that shit. It's a total bore-fest.'

'No, it's not, just wait.' Mac hates all social media and unlike most people, he has no online profile at all. I should know; I've looked.

I find Katarina's profile and hold it up to show Mac.

'Look,' I say.

Mac stares at the screen and then looks at me.

'It's a picture of you.' He looks at me blankly and I grin. 'What?' he asks.

'It's not me,' I say.

'Of course it's you,' Mac says, with a frown.

'No, it's not. It's my double. I've got a double.'

Mac takes the phone from my hand and studies the screen, scrolling through Katarina's *Instagram* posts.

'They say everyone has a double and I've met mine,' I say. 'How cool is that?'

Mac doesn't speak but continues scrolling, clicking on pictures and reading her posts. I fill him in on how I saw her and snooped her *Instagram* account while she was sitting in front of me and feel rather pleased with myself. I don't tell him that I thought that there must be some way I could use our likeness to my advantage because I don't want to look like a complete idiot.

'So,' I say, starting to get bored as he continues to hog my phone. 'She looks just like me, doesn't she?'

'Yeah,' he agrees. 'She does. Spitting image.'

He screenshots her profile and sends the picture to his own phone before handing my mobile back to me. He stares at me for a moment unsmilingly and I feel the undercurrent of danger in him that I felt the first time I met him.

'Why did you do that?' I ask.

He snakes his arm around my waist and pulls me towards him.

'I'm going to find out where she lives,' he says, brushing my hair back from my face.

'Why?' My stomach flips as he kisses me gently on the lips.

He smiles and kisses me again and pulls me closer and doesn't answer.

I know why.

He's planning something.

CHAPTER THREE

'I don't want it, Mum,' I say, for the third time.

'Why not? I don't want nothing for it. You can have it for free.' She holds out the dress to me and I reluctantly take it. I have two exactly like it in the wardrobe and I never wear either of them. She stole those ones, too, and she's only giving this one to me because no one will buy it off her because it's so horrible. If she's going to nick stuff she could at least try and get something decent that people actually want. It's probably from the rail nearest the exit and so was easy to grab and make a quick getaway.

Mum pulls a chair out from the table and sits down.

'I don't know, most kids would be pleased if their Mum give 'em a dress and wouldn't be so bloody ungrateful,' she says, pulling a crumpled packet of *Lambert and Butler* out of the pocket of her jeans. She pulls a cigarette out of the packet and clamps it between her lips.

'Mum, please, not in here.'

She ignores me and lights the cigarette with a yellow plastic lighter.

'Oh, give over and open the window,' she says, eyes narrowed, between puffs. 'It's only a bit of smoke.'

I lean over the kitchen sink and push the window open as wide as it will go and then go over to the kitchen door and close it.

'You never used to mind,' she says, accusingly.

I sigh but say nothing. I've always minded but never used to bother saying anything because she ignores me anyway, just as she has today. Mac can't stand the smell of cigarette smoke and says only working-class people smoke nowadays. He meant it as an insult when he said it because he makes no secret of the fact that he doesn't like Mum, even though he's only met her a few times. I don't blame him; I don't like her much either and she's my mother.

He doesn't consider himself working-class; he speaks and dresses well and I must be a snob because I like that he thinks of me the same way. He says just because we're born poor doesn't mean we have to stay that way.

'So, talking of arseholes,' Mum says, even though we weren't. 'Where's that bloke of yours?' She exhales a long plume of grey smoke straight into my face. She likes Mac about as much as he likes her which is not at all.

'He's away,' I say, batting away the smoke with

my hand. 'And don't call him an arsehole.'

'He's always *away*, ain't he?' she says, with a sneer. 'What does he actually *do* anyway?'

I sigh. No way do I want to tell her that I don't actually know. When I ask, Mac answers with *helping on a refit for a few days* or *house-moving*. He's never actually told me exactly what he does and I don't ask anymore because the last time I asked he told me I was turning into a nag. Two things he hates in a woman; nagging and being needy. He's assured me it's nothing to do with drugs and that's good enough for me.

'He's up north on a re-fit,' I lie.

Mum sniffs and sucks deeply on her *Lambert and Butler*.

'Sounds dodgy to me.' She exhales noisily. 'You don't get a flash car like his doing re-fits. You want to watch him, there's something about him I don't trust.'

'Really?' I stare at her, straight-faced. 'You're calling Mac dodgy when you've been shop-lifting since before I was born?'

She bristles and won't look at me.

'Least you've always known where I am,' she eventually says, dropping her still lit cigarette into the dregs of her coffee where it sizzles and gives off a smell even more disgusting than when it was lit.

'I know exactly where he is,' I lie. 'And I trust him completely.'

Mum sniffs again but doesn't comment. She pulls another cigarette from the packet but when she sees the look on my face, she pushes it back in.

'And what about Seamus?' I ask. 'He's hardly a catch, is he? He's a drug dealer and layabout and well dodgy. Do you trust him?'

'He's not a drug dealer,' she protests. 'He just sorts his friends out with a bit here and there, doing them a favour.'

'Oh, that's alright then. I'm sure the judge will go easy on him if he tells him that when he gets caught,' I say, sarcastically.

'You can say what you like about him, I don't care, I know I can trust him when push comes to shove. And I'm only asking because I care,' she says, in a wheedling tone, confirming my suspicion as to the reason for her visit and the gift of the stolen dress.

She wants something.

She doesn't care about me and she never really has done. She let slip when she was five vodka and lemons deep one night that she would have had an abortion when she found out she was pregnant with me but it was too late, she was over the time-limit for a termination.

I was twelve at the time.

I wasn't surprised; she'd never made any secret of the fact that I'd ruined her life although what she thinks she'd have achieved without me, God knows. But to her credit, she kept a roof over my head and sort of looked after me until I could fend for myself so I can't feel too sorry for myself. There's plenty around here that have had far worse an upbringing than me – although she made it quite clear that she wanted me out of her flat and into one of my own as soon as I turned eighteen. Luckily, getting a flat on this estate isn't at all difficult because only the lowest of the low want to live here. Well, they don't *want* to live here, obviously, but they have no choice. There are plenty of empty flats going begging in this block all the time because it's such a rough area and the flats are shabby and damp. I could have just squatted in one and saved myself some rent but unlike Mum, I'd rather be legal and pay rent to the council than a drug dealer who fancies himself as a gangster landlord.

'What do you want?' I ask.

Mum looks up at me with her once pretty blue eyes with what she thinks is an innocent look.

'What makes you think I want something?' she asks.

'Seamus kicked you out again?'

'No,' she says, indignantly. 'It's my flat, he can't kick me out.'

I snort but stay silent. I'm relieved, I don't want her staying here for days on end because I wouldn't really be able to say no because she is my mum, when all said and done. If Mum's here I think Mac will go and stay somewhere else because he won't be able to tolerate her and she'll make no effort to be anything other than her annoying self. Mum might say it's her flat but Seamus has kicked her out loads of times; he bolts the door from the inside and sits in there stinking, drinking and smoking weed until he comes out of his foul mood and lets her back in. So even though it's Mum's flat, try telling him that.

'What then?'

'Well.' She squirms in her chair and looks longingly at her cigarettes lying on the table. 'I'm a bit short for the rent this month.'

'Are you?' I say. 'Well, maybe Seamus can put his hand in his pocket instead of sponging off you. He does live there.'

'He's a bit short too 'cos he had to pay his fine.'

I roll my eyes and sigh. Mum frowns.

'Sorry, Mum, no can do. I'm not working and I've only got my benefit to live on. I've got nothing to give you.'

She looks up at me and narrows her eyes.

'*He's* always loaded, though, ain't he? That Mac. Couldn't you ask him for some cash?'

She doesn't miss a trick; even though Mac has never flashed the cash in front of her, he *has* always got plenty and somehow, she knows although I certainly haven't told her. I swear to God she can smell it.

'No, I couldn't,' I say. 'I pay my own way and I'm certainly not asking him for money for you. Go without fags for a few days, that'll pay the rent as well as giving your lungs a rest.'

She stands up abruptly, pushing the chair backwards, the legs making a screeching sound on the lino.

'Okay miss hoity-toity, there's no need to speak to me like you're a bloody school teacher. You're no better than I am so just remember that and mind your manners.' She snatches the dress from my hands and picks her cigarettes up from the table and stuffs them into her pocket along with the lighter.

'Just don't come asking me for help any time soon,' she spits at me as she stomps towards the door. 'Because you're on your own.'

She yanks the kitchen door open and I hear her stamping down the hallway to the front door. There's the sound of the door being opened and a crash as it's flung against the wall. I brace myself for the bang of it closing and sure enough, seconds later, the kitchen shakes as Mum hurls the door shut.

That'll be the last I see of her for another week.

Thankfully.

* * *

I was nervous about washing my hair; I thought there was no way I'd be able to replicate the style that Alun had done but surprisingly, by the time I put the hairdryer down it looks just as good as when I walked out of the salon. I'd put off washing it for as long as possible but it got to the point where I couldn't leave it any longer.

I pull on a pair of black Lycra leggings with a slim-fitting sports top and look at myself in the mirror. I look hot, and I'm not being big-headed, I'm just stating a fact. I'm slim and have a good figure and although I have no intention of going to the gym even though I'm wearing sports gear, I will be doing exercise of a sort later on.

Mac's coming home today.

I can't wait to see him and although I hate it when he's away, the sex is always explosive when we haven't seen each for a few days. He's been away for nearly a week this time and I was starting to panic that he wasn't going to come back.

WhatsApps are always sporadic when he's away and he rarely calls because he says he has to concentrate on the job and can't be distracted by me. Even though I know this and it's always this way, all sorts of rubbish still keeps going through my mind. What if he's met someone else and he never comes back? He met me when he was on a job and sometimes, I can't help wondering if he has a girl in all the other places he works.

Wherever they are.

Because, let's face it, I don't know a lot about Mac. If I ask him about his parents or family, he dismisses them with *haven't seen them for years* and the only friends of his that I've met are the ones he was with the night I met him, and I never actually spoke to any of them. It's my own fault; when he came up to me in the crowded club on the night we met, I took one look at him and couldn't believe that he was talking to me when he could have had any girl in that club. I'm attractive but there are lots of girls hotter than me but he chose *me*.

I saw him before he saw me and was admiring him from the other side of the bar when he turned to pick up his drink and noticed me looking at him. He stared at me unsmilingly and my heart was racing as I stared back; I felt locked in his gaze and I couldn't move. After what felt like hours but was only minutes, he slowly put his drink down and walked around the bar towards me. I couldn't take my eyes off him the whole time and as he walked slowly up to me, I thought I was going to pass out because I could barely breathe. He stood in front of me and I felt such an idiot because I was like a rabbit caught in the headlights. His eyes searched my face and he had such an intense expression that I thought I was going to faint. And then suddenly his face broke into a smile and he said *do you come here often* and we both laughed because it was so corny. He bought me a drink and we stood at the bar and talked but I don't even remember what we talked about.

I never did drink my Malibu and Coke.

I don't usually do one night stands because I just end up feeling shit and used but Mac was different; when he came back to my flat at the end of the night it seemed like the most natural thing in the world. Somehow, I knew that he'd be sticking around and not disappearing as fast as he could. He wanted to know everything about me, everywhere I'd been and everything I'd ever done;

which didn't take long because I've been nowhere and done nothing. He's generous too; if we go out, he won't let me pay and he insists on giving me money because he says he's practically living here even though he's always away. And if he's secretive and doesn't divulge much about his life, that's okay because I trust him totally.

I think.

The sound of the front door opening and closing alerts me to the fact that Mac is home. I quickly check my appearance in the bedroom mirror and then go out into the lounge.

'Mac!' I cross the room and throw myself into his arms and he hugs me tightly.

'Ugh,' I say, when he releases his hold on me. 'You're soaking.'

'It's chucking it down.' He shrugs his jacket off and drapes it over the back of a chair. 'That's all it does in this country; fucking rain.'

I pick his coat up and take it into the bathroom and hang it from the shower rail where it drips into the bath.

'Never mind, you're dry now and I'll warm you up,' I say, when I return to the lounge. He's already stretched out on the sofa with the TV remote in his hand and I settle down next to him and he puts his arm around me and pulls me close.

'The sooner we can leave this shithole of a country and go somewhere hot and sunny, the better,' he says, quietly.

We, he said we! I snuggle into his arms and

imagine us lying on a beach soaking up the sun.

'You'd better get yourself a passport,' he says quietly. 'Because I don't know how much longer I can stand it here.'

I ease myself out of his arms, jump up from the sofa and dash into the bedroom.

'What are you doing?' Mac shouts.

I don't answer but open the top drawer of the chest of drawers and pull out the envelope that arrived yesterday and take out my brand new passport. I applied for it but never told Mac; I was hoping that we might book a holiday abroad and I didn't want the lack of a passport to stop me. Mac's been to loads of places and when I told him I've never been abroad he couldn't believe it; he said he thought that everyone in the world had at least been to Benidorm.

It was a right rigmarole getting the passport as well as costing a fortune; I saved up some of the cash that Mac's been giving me every week to pay for it otherwise I wouldn't have been able to afford it. I had to get my doctor to sign my photograph and he had the bloody cheek to charge me for it, as if they don't earn enough money. It doesn't matter now though and it was all worth it because Mac wants me to go with him. I rush out of the bedroom and stand in front of him.

'Ta-da!' I say, waving my passport at him.

'You've got a passport?' he asks, looking puzzled. 'I thought you said you'd never been abroad?'

'I haven't,' I say, opening it and showing him the

photograph. 'I've just got it. It's brand, spanking, new.'

His face slowly breaks into a grin and he leans towards me and takes hold of my hand and pulls me down onto his lap. He takes the passport from me and opens it and studies it.

'Well,' he says, with a grin. 'Aren't you full of surprises.'

CHAPTER FOUR

Mac's found out where Katarina lives.

Listen to me; I talk about her as if I know her, how weird am I? But in a way I do feel I know her because her whole life is on *Instagram* and she makes no attempt to hide it. Every day I check her account to see what she's been doing and she posts *everything,* I even know what her favourite foods are because she's always posting pictures of what she has for dinner. I don't get people who do that; why? Why would you want the world to know everything about you? I rarely post anything; I just *like* other people's stuff. The only thing I'd like to post is a picture of Mac and I but he's told me that no way am I to put *any* pictures of him on any sort of social media and by the look on his face when he said it, I know he meant it.

Infuriatingly, although Mac knows where Katarina lives, he won't tell me how he found out, just that *he knows people.* He told me this just as I was leaving the house to go and sign on and I'm now sitting in the Jobcentre wanting answers to questions that I can't ask him until I get home. I wanted to stay and find out more but I daren't be late today in case they stop my benefits. The snotty cow who I saw last time definitely didn't believe that I'd been actively looking for work – I haven't, obviously – and I have to take proof this time to show what jobs I've applied for.

I think Mac did it on purpose because we'd spent practically the whole morning together – most of it in bed – so he had plenty of time to tell me before I had to go out. He does like to wind me up and tease me and I know that he won't tell me anything until he's good and ready. He knew I'd be itching to find out all the details. I did think about asking him to give me a lift in his car so we could talk about it on the way but I stopped myself. Not because he'd say no, but because I hate coming here and I couldn't bear the thought of being dropped at the doors of the Jobcentre with all of the weird men that hang around outside watching me. God knows why they choose to hang around outside smoking and watching everyone; there have got to be better places to do that. Maybe they get a kick out of the fact that everyone who goes into the Jobcentre has to fight their way through them. There are two beefy security guards inside the doors who stare at me menacingly as I go in. They pull me aside and remind me that it's zero tolerance on abuse of the staff and then they tell me to take my mask off. I argue that I always wear a mask and have a perfect right to but they say take it off or leave. So I take it off.

Why don't they go outside and tell the weirdos hanging around out there to leave? They're too frightened, that's why, and it's easier to bully and intimidate people like me. I should have bought Mac with me; they wouldn't have dared to ask if he'd been here. As well as being tall and powerful looking, when he chooses Mac has a quiet coldness about him that makes people think twice about crossing him.

'Jessica Atkins?'

I look up when I hear my name to see the same woman who interviewed me last time standing at the front of the room. Just my luck; I could tell she didn't like me one bit and I don't suppose it's going to go any better this time.

I stand up and saunter over to her, deliberately taking my time. I can see by her pursed lips and frown that she's not amused but I don't care. If she's going to make life difficult for me – which I'm sure she will – I'm not going to make it easy for her. I follow her down a corridor with scuffed walls and tatty carpet repaired with bright yellow gaffer tape and into a small cubicle with a desk inside it. There is no door on the cubicle and I can hear the muted sound of other people's conversations as I take a seat in front of her desk.

'So, Jessica,' she says, once she's settled herself behind the desk. 'My name is Beatrice and before I ask you to sign to say that you've not been working and would like to claim benefit, we need to discuss your efforts to find work.'

I say nothing and sit back in the chair; let her do all the work.

'So.' She looks down at the paperwork in front of her. 'What have you been doing to actively seek employment?'

'I've applied for lots of jobs,' I say. 'And I've been actively searching for vacancies online every day.'

'Have you filled in all the details on your activity history sheet?'

'Yes,' I say, pulling out the sheet of paper from my pocket and unfolding it.

She raises an eyebrow as I lay it on the desk and attempt to smooth out the creases before handing it over to her. She takes it from me and reads it.

It's basically a list of the times every day that I've spend looking for a job and the details of any that I've applied for.

'And you have proof that you've applied for these jobs?'

'Yeah,' I say. 'Although it's all on my phone because they were online applications. I can show you, if you like.'

She purses her lips.

'You should have used the computers at the job club to print out your applications and then you could have brought the copies with you.'

'Couldn't afford the bus fare,' I say, with a shrug.

'Could you show me, please?' she asks.

'Yeah.' I scroll through my phone, find the acknowledgements of the applications and pass the phone to her.

We sit in silence while she studies them. Why did I have to get her? I know people that come here that have never worked a day in their life and no one asks them to prove they're looking for a job. My neighbour, Ted, is forty-three and he's never had a job since the day he left school and he proudly boasts this to anyone who'll listen. He says he's not bending to the system because he's a free spirit who doesn't want to be tied to a soul-destroying job. Or, in other words, he's just lazy. What I'd like to know is why is he allowed to loaf around for years while I'm not?

Beatrice holds my phone out across the desk and I take it from her and tuck it in my pocket.

'I see,' she says. 'That you've applied for a position as a PA, a receptionist and an administrator. Is that right?'

'Yep.'

Beatrice sighs and taps a few keys on her keyboard and studies the screen.

'Yet you're not actually qualified for any of those jobs, are you?'

I shrug.

'What was your last period of employment as?'

'Temporary Christmas staff,' I say. 'At the supermarket.'

'A checkout operator?'

'Store colleague,' I correct.

She does the lip pursing thing again. 'As I just said, you were a checkout operator, which begs the question; why have you applied for jobs that you're not qualified for?'

'I want to better myself, don't I?'

Obviously, I've applied for them because I don't want there to be any possibility at all of actually getting any of them. Beatrice knows this as well as I do.

She stares at me and I stare back at her without blinking. Tell me I'm a liar, I mentally taunt her, go on, just say it.

She doesn't. She eventually looks away from me and at her screen for a few moments before looking down at the desk and flicking through my file. She pulls a sheet of paper out and pushes it across the desk to me.

'Sign and date there, please.' She practically throws a cheap biro at me.

I pick the pen up and scribble my name and date on the declaration and pass the paper back to her.

'Come back in two weeks,' she mutters. 'And I expect to see evidence that you've applied for employment that you're actually capable of doing otherwise I'll have to put your case forward for a review.'

I stand up and walk out of the cubicle without speaking.

A review. That means they'll stop my benefit for sure if I can't prove I've really been looking for work – which means I'll get a job because there are hundreds of crap job vacancies that I'm perfectly qualified for.

What a bitch.

Although looking on the bright side, that means I have two more weeks of freedom before I have to go and work at a dead end job that barely pays more than my benefits. I might as well enjoy it while I can. I burst out of the Jobcentre doors into bright sunshine and try and ignore the leers and mutterings from the weirdos as I fight my way through them and the fug of cigarette smoke.

At least Mac is waiting for me at home.

As I speed walk to the bus station, I wonder how long it'll be before Mac and I can escape to a new life in the sun. How much money do we actually *need*?

I veer around the corner just as my bus pulls away; now I have to wait another ten minutes for the next one. I stand by the cigarette kiosk and wait. There are benches to sit on but they're grubby and God knows what filth is on them.

I bet Katarina has never had to catch a bus in her life. I bet she's never had to sign on for benefits or explain herself to a snooty Jobcentre clerk who thinks they have a right to tell everyone what to do just because they're sitting behind a desk.

I try to imagine what it would be like to never have to sign on again, to have money, to live somewhere hot and sunny with Mac but the stink of diesel fumes keeps me firmly in the present.

One day we'll have our dream of a life in the sun.

But one day is no good.
I want it now.

* * *

'You're not going to tell me anything? Not even how you found out where she lives?'

Mac smirks; the same annoying smirk that he's had since I got home.

'Some things you don't need to know,' he says, pointing the remote at the TV and flicking channels until he finds a football match. 'Some things you're better off *not* knowing.'

I love him so much but sometimes I could truthfully hit him, like right now. I sit back on the sofa and cross my arms and sigh.

'I can't see the point, anyway,' I say, trying hard not to sulk.

'What do you mean?'

'Well,' I say. 'I might have someone who looks just like me but what use is that? What can I get out of it?'

He turns from watching the TV and looks at me.

'Well, I can hardly walk into her bank and ask the cashier to hand over wads of cash to me just because I look like her, can I?' I say. 'It's not actually much use if I don't have her credit cards and stuff, in fact why do I even need to look like her because anyone can get their hands on her money if they have the right cards and everything.'

Mac stares at me for a moment and then starts

to laugh.

'What's so funny?' I demand.

'You,' he says. 'How can you be such an innocent living on an estate like this? Christ, everyone who lives here is either fiddling benefits or working some scam. Your mother's a professional shoplifter, her boyfriend's a drug dealer, how can you be so straight? There are *so* many ways we can use this.'

I'm not an innocent even though Mac thinks I am. I'm aware that most people I know are fiddling in one way or another but I still can't see how looking like Katarina is of any benefit. There are plenty of ways to steal from someone and none of them involve having a double. I'm rare in that I'm not involved in any criminal behaviour but that doesn't mean I don't know anything about it. I've spent my life avoiding ending up like my mother but it's not because I think I'm better than anyone else around here but because I don't want to stay here forever doing small-time crime living a small-time life.

Not that I've ever had any idea how to get out of here, but I *do* know that if I have to do something illegal it's got to be big and worthwhile enough to risk my liberty.

'But how?' I ask.

Mac laughs even more and I feel foolish because there must be something obvious that I'm missing. I say nothing but wait for him to stop laughing and tell me how having a double can possibly benefit us.

But he doesn't.

When he stops laughing, he simply turns away from me and continues watching TV. I sit for a moment, feeling like a complete fool and then Mac puts his arm around my shoulders and pulls me towards him and holds me tightly.

'That's what I love about you,' he says, kissing the top of my head. 'You haven't got a nasty bone in your body.'

I stay immobile in his arms and wonder.

Did he just say that he loved me?

CHAPTER FIVE

Okay, so Mac never actually said the words I love you but he almost said it and actions speak louder than words, don't they? He's got a plan, although he never said exactly what it was but he did eventually tell me a little of it, so that means that he trusts me and he's serious about us moving to Spain.

We stayed sitting on the sofa watching TV – well Mac was, I wasn't really paying attention – and when the programme finished, he started to tell me about Katarina.

He said that her house is in Hampstead and it's an Edwardian semi-detached with three-stories and bay-windows, although he didn't tell me how he found this out. He noticed the disappointment on my face when he said this because I'd imagined her living in some sort of mansion and a semi-detached was a bit of a let-down. He said don't let the fact that it's a semi fool you because he'd done a search on the internet for it on a website that shows what houses were sold for and it was last sold three years ago for three-and-a-half-million pounds. It has seven bedrooms and a large garden and it's in Hampstead village, he said, as if that meant something to me. You have to have plenty of money to live there, he said, because it's an upmarket and sought after place.

He said he drove around the street a few times and had a good look around the area to get a feel for the place so he can plan what he's going to do next. He said there was a skip outside the front of the house with old bathroom bits and rubbish in it so obviously they've been having some work done to the house.

He says his plan is to scout the place out and find out what their routine is so that he can get inside and find Katarina's passport, bank cards and stuff and take photographs of it all. He doesn't plan to steal any of it as all that will happen is that she'll cancel all her cards and she'll be on alert for someone ripping her off. He says having all her information without her knowledge will be far more useful than stealing the actual cards or passport. Besides, he said, who needs the real thing when it's so easy to clone stuff. It's like having the real thing without them *knowing* that you have it.

I felt a bit alarmed when he said about getting in to her house because I don't want him getting caught and being sent to prison. He laughed loudly and said no way would he get caught, he's far too careful and besides, he wasn't going to break in, he was going to get into and out of the house without anyone knowing that he'd been there. A break-in would set alarm bells ringing and that was to be avoided at all costs.

I must admit that he spoke so confidently about it that I couldn't help being impressed by him and he made it sound so easy. I asked him how he could be so sure of himself and he asked what did I think he was doing all the time he was away?

Re-fits, I suggested, or house-moving?

He smiled and said that it was good that I thought of him that way but the reality was that getting into Katarina's house wouldn't be a new thing for him and it wouldn't be risky at all because he was good at what he did.

I wasn't surprised but it was still a shock to hear him actually say it, because I know that he's better than the men that live round here; he's got class. But the stark reality is that he's a thief, just like most of the people on this estate.

He's just the same as Mum.

But I'm not disappointed; or maybe I am just a bit, but I know that for us to start a new life in Spain, unless we win the lottery we're going to have to break the law and do something *big*, otherwise we'll be stuck here forever. But the risk with doing something big is that if we get caught, the consequences will be worse.

But I won't think about that, because it's pointless.

I've never thought I was better than anyone else

– not even Mum, who thinks that I look down on her – I've always known that I'm just the same as everyone else. The difference between me and them is that I want to do something that'll make a real difference to my life; not live hand to mouth selling on cheap shoplifted clothes from *Primark* or *Matalan* to whoever will buy them.

Mac hasn't told me what part I have to play in this plan that he's cooking up but he has said that I have to believe in myself and have confidence. He says that being confident is everything; if you're sure of yourself and show no nerves then people don't question you, they don't doubt you if you behave as if you have the perfect right to do anything.

I have to start believing in myself and believe that I can do whatever he asks of me or it's never going to work.

I just hope what he has planned is going to happen soon because in less than two weeks' time I have to sign on, which means I have to apply for a shit job that I'm going to get. I'm impatient; I just want to do whatever needs doing and start our new life in Spain.

We talked about it a lot over the four days he was back but he never told me anything new so I just have to accept that he'll tell me the details when I need to know. He did say that I need to look at Katarina's *Instagram* account every day so that we can see if she has any holidays planned or anything that will mean she's going to be away from the house. I said I would but I didn't tell him that I already look every day; sometimes every hour. She details every minute and detail of her life on there and I can't help looking to see what new thing she's done. Yesterday she went to a fabulous spa in the Cotswolds and I felt sick with envy at all the selfies of her looking glamorous by the indoor pool.

I so want her life.

She'd even got the beauty therapist to take a picture of her while she was lying on a bed with a face mask on. She captioned it k*eep young and beautiful if you want to be loved* and she also hash tagged all the beauty products the spa uses so she probably gets all of the products for free.

She wouldn't have time for a job because she must spend half of her life taking photographs to put on *Instagram*. I looked back over her old posts and she documents *everything.*

A picture of power tools and buckets and assorted builder's clutter was captioned; *The builders are done!* Followed by *bathrooms complete!* This was followed by numerous selfies of her posing in the mirrors of four different bathrooms. Four bathrooms! I'd like just one decent one that didn't have damp all around the window and a shower with all the power of a dripping tap.

The more I look the more I want her life and the more dissatisfied I become with my own. Looking at her *Instagram* every day is going to give me the nerve to go through with whatever Mac has planned because she has *so* much. I'm assuming what Mac has planned is fraud, because what else can it be? And I'm refusing to feel bad about it because whatever we steal from her, it won't be like stealing from someone who doesn't have very much. It's not as if we're actually going to hurt her.

Anyway, I can't actually stop looking at her *Instagram* even if I wanted to because I've become obsessed with the woman with my face who has the life that I want. The first thing I do every morning is to log on to see what she's posted but at least I have a reason to be obsessed; there are plenty of people obsessed with celebrities who watch their every move so I'm not as sad as them.

Anyway, it's research.

When Mac left yesterday, he didn't say how long he'd be gone – he never does – and he wouldn't say if this time he was going to *pay a visit to Katarina's house*, as he puts it, or if that would be another time so I guess I'm only going to know after he's done it. He says he doesn't like to talk about when he's doing stuff in case he jinxes it; he's superstitious about things like that. So I didn't ask and I didn't nag and I didn't ask when he'd be back. But after he'd kissed me goodbye and left the flat, I went over to the window and stood there until I saw him come out. And as I watched him climbing into his car down in the car park, I made a wish.

Make it happen soon.

* * *

I picked up a pizza from the Co-op for my dinner tonight. I could have gone to Asda and bought one for half the price but that would have meant getting on a bus which would have cost me nearly two pounds so I wouldn't have saved much and it would have taken twice as long to get there.

I could have walked there; I *should* have walked there because it's not as if I've got anything else to do but I simply couldn't be bothered. I've noticed that I'm like this when Mac's not here; I feel at a loose end and I can't be bothered to cook anything decent to eat and I just want to stuff my face with carbs and chocolate. I don't do that when he's here because I don't want him to think I'm a lazy, greedy cow who's going to turn into a big fat slob if she's not careful. I'll be fine by tomorrow and back to normal eating – not least because I'm never sure whether he's going to turn up early whereas I know I'm safe tonight. He only left yesterday and he's always stayed away for at least two nights so I'm pretty certain he's not going to catch me pigging out later on.

Mum's been texting me for the last couple of days so I'm going to call in on her on the way home. Not because I want to, but because if I don't, she'll just turn up unannounced at my flat and stink the place out with her cigarettes. At least if I go to hers, I don't have to stay very long whereas if she comes to mine, she'll stay for hours and hours no matter how much I hint for her to leave. She's obviously forgiven me for being *hoity-toity* as she puts it, the other day. She can never bear a grudge for very long, not least because her memory is getting worse by the day and she often can't remember what or why she was pissed off with me in the first place. I think that years of a daily diet of forty *Lambert and Butler* and cheap vodka has started to addle her brain. The fact that Seamus smokes weed constantly doesn't help either, her flat is so full of his weed smoke that she might as well smoke it herself.

I hope Seamus isn't there; he rarely speaks to me but he leers and watches me and makes me feel uncomfortable. God knows what Mum sees in him; bald with horrible hooded eyes he's about as attractive as Gollum. Hopefully he'll be down at the *George and Dragon* boosting their profits as he seems to spend most of his waking hours there.

I push open the door into *Titan House* and walk straight past the lift and along to the doors to the stairs. Mum is on the third floor but no way am I getting in the lift to go up there; if she lived on the tenth floor, I would still take the stairs. I never take the lift, not even in my own block. Even if they're working – which they're quite often not – I never use them as first of all they stink of piss as they're used as toilets, but also because they're a favourite place for getting mugged. Or worse. The muggers or gropers are always in twos and they watch and wait out of sight until someone gets into the lift and then they jump into the lift quickly before the doors close. You're stuck in there with them until the lift doors eventually open. Their usual victims are women because they don't put up much resistance and hand over their purses without a fight because it's preferable to getting raped.

As I climb the stairs, I wonder what Mum wants; probably money, because she'll have forgotten that she asked me for some last week. I reach the third floor and console myself with the fact that at least the stairs will work off some of the pizza that I'm going to eat later. I walk briskly along the corridor and knock on her door, avoiding the sharp edges of the peeling paint.

I probably should have told her I was coming in case she's out shop-lifting although as it's nearly five-o'clock she should be in because it's too late for stealing; the shops aren't busy enough.

The door is yanked open and Mum stares at me blankly, a cigarette dangling from the corner of her mouth.

'What you doing 'ere?' she asks.

'Thought I'd come and see my mother,' I say, dryly.

'You should 'ave let me know,' she says, with a frown. 'Cos I might have been out.'

'You're not though, are you?' I say, as I step into the hallway and follow her down the grubby hallway to the lounge. The hallway smells of fried food, cigarette smoke and vinegar.

I'm relieved to see that Seamus isn't here and I flop down onto the sofa and kick off my shoes. Mum sits down opposite me and stubs her dog-end out in the ash tray before immediately lighting up another cigarette.

'So what did you want?' I ask.

She takes a long drag on her cigarette before answering.

'That's bloody charming,' she says, between puffs. 'Do you need a reason to come and see your mother?'

I shrug and bat the smoke away that she's just exhaled in my direction.

'You're in a funny mood today,' she says.

'No I'm not.' I am, though, she's right.

'Don't know if I'm going to tell you now,' she says, with a scowl.

I stand up and slip my feet into my shoes.

'Oh, bloody hell,' she says. 'You've really got one on you. Sit down. I need to talk to you.'

I study her for a moment and sit down on the edge of the sofa. She can say whatever crap it is she has to say and I'm going. I am *so* not in the mood for her and I wish I hadn't come here now.

'I've heard some rumours and I thought it only right that you should know,' she says, speaking as if she's giving evidence at a trial.

'Get on with it, Mum,' I say.

'Right. Well, it's about him, that arsehole you're living with.'

I stand up.

'I'm going Mum because I don't want to hear whatever crap you're going to come out with. And stop calling him an arsehole.'

'It's not crap,' she says. 'Shani down the club told me and she's never wrong about people.'

'I don't care,' I say. 'I know you don't like him but that's your problem. I don't like Seamus but you don't take any notice of anything I say about him, do you?'

'That's different,' she says. 'I'm your mum and I have to look out for you. I don't want to see you get hurt.'

I almost believe her for a moment and then I see the glint in her eye and I remember that she doesn't really care and never has done, she just loves to gossip. Every word I utter will be relayed back to Shani at the club and then broadcast to every punter who walks through the door.

'Anyway,' she says. 'It's not that I don't like him, he doesn't like me. He looks down on me and you've started doing the same. I don't trust him. He's shifty.'

I stare down at her and say nothing.

'And he talks funny and he's stuck up,' she adds.

'He doesn't talk funny.' I sigh. 'He speaks well and that doesn't make him shifty or stuck up.'

'There you go,' Mum snorts. 'You're even starting to sound like him...'

'I'm going,' I say, heading for the door.

'Shani says when he's away he's not doing re-fits or nothing...'

'Not listening,' I call over my shoulder as I head down the hallway.

I hear her footsteps scuttling along behind me

and as I yank open the front door Mum is so close behind that she nearly falls into me.

'He's lying to you and you need to listen to me. I'm only telling you 'cos I care,' she wheedles.

I ignore her and walk down the corridor towards the stairs.

'You'll wish you'd listened to me...' she calls after me, as I step into the stairwell and head down the stairs. It's laughable that she thinks she's protecting me; she has no idea that I already know what Mac is up to but there's no way I'm going to tell her because she'll blab it to everyone down the club.

The working men's club. What a laugh; none of them have ever worked a day in their lives.

I burst out of the exit door and into light drizzle that's begun to fall. Wonderful, now I'm going to be soaking wet as well as pissed off when I get home. Too late I realise that I've left the pizza I bought in Mum's flat; there's no way I'm going back there to get it. A vision of Seamus chomping into it with his big rubbery lips pops into my head and I want to scream.

I feel like bursting into tears and I finally admit to myself what's really been bothering me all day.

I think I'm pregnant.

CHAPTER SIX

I open my eyes and stare up at the damp stain on the bedroom ceiling.

I haven't slept well and I know that there's no way around it; I need to buy a pregnancy test. I've been hoping and praying that my period will start but it's now seven days late and I need to know for sure. Seven days may be nothing to most women but to me it's ominous; I'm never late, *never*; even one day late is unheard of for me.

I'm on the pill so it shouldn't even be possible because it's not as if I've forgotten to take it or anything stupid like that because I'm always very careful. The sight of girls barely out of school pushing buggies around the precinct has always stuck in my mind because no way do I want to end up like that. It's only now that I'm late that I recall that a couple of weeks ago I drank far too much on a night out and spent the night throwing up. I'm guessing that this has made the pill ineffective.

The annoying thing is that I'm not even a

drinker; Mum has succeeded in putting me off alcohol for life. Mac and I went on a rare night out to a club in town and I drank quite a few cocktails as Mac likes them and he doesn't like to drink alone. They don't taste as if they even have any alcohol in them and that's why I drank so many. I was fine until we left the club; once we got outside the fresh air hit me and that was it. We got a cab back home and I had to have the window open and practically hang my head out of it to stop myself from throwing up all over the seats.

Mac thought it was hilarious and called me a lightweight but I felt like death by the time I'd finished throwing up in the toilet. I felt awful the next day, too.

So now I've gone and ruined everything.

I'll have to buy a pregnancy test and find out for sure which means I'll have to get the bus into town. No way can I buy one at one of the shops around here; some nosey sod is bound to see me and before you can say *condom* it'll be all around the estate that I'm pregnant. I close my eyes and promise myself that I'll get out of bed in exactly one minute and brave the freezing run to the bathroom. It may be March but this flat is as damp and cold as it was in December. Without Mac here to keep me warm I've had to resort to wearing socks to bed.

Mac.

I haven't heard from him since he left.

Four whole days without so much as a message

or a phone call.

He's never done that before, not contacted me at all. He never messages very much when he's away but he's never not messaged at all. The first WhatsApp message that I sent him has been read but the three I've sent since haven't.

I'm really worried.

What if he's had an accident and is lying in a hospital somewhere in a coma? How would I even know?

I wouldn't.

Or maybe he's been arrested trying to break into Katarina's house.

Or maybe he's had enough of me and he's never coming back. Maybe he has another woman. So much for me thinking that he loved me.

All of these things are possible and it's made me realise how little I know about him. All I have is his phone number which isn't any good if he doesn't answer my messages. I don't even know exactly where he lives. When I've asked him, he said that he has a room in a house-share with four other people on the outskirts of London but it's a dump and he only keeps it so he has somewhere to store his stuff. I don't even have an address.

Which is weird, isn't it?

It all seemed perfectly reasonable when we were talking about it but now, I think I should have been more insistent about details in case I needed to get hold of him urgently.

I keep trying to tell myself that it's not weird

that I don't know a lot about him but I can't seem to convince myself. I have no way of contacting him and he could disappear from my life and I wouldn't be able to find him. He's not on any social media so I wouldn't be able to track him down that way, either. I'm trying not to panic at the thought of never seeing him again and I keep telling myself that there's an explanation for his radio silence but I can't actually think of one.

His clothes are hanging in the wardrobe next to mine and his toothbrush is in the bathroom but nothing else of any use in finding him is here; I have nothing that can tell me where he is.

I wish I had someone to talk to about it but I don't. I have friends of course, but truthfully, although I've known Taylor and Dani all my life and we went to school together, we're not close. We only really bother with one another when we're between boyfriends which would have been a lot of the time for me before I met Mac but not for Taylor and Dani, they always have a bloke on the go. Taylor has a daughter, too, so we have even less in common.

I could tell them about Mac being away and being afraid that I'm pregnant and I know they'd sympathise with me. But I also know that they'd gossip about it to their other friends and the whole estate would soon know everything about my life. Which is why I don't tell anyone anything, because I don't trust them to keep their mouths shut, not even my own mother.

I have trust issues.

Except when it comes to Mac; because I've trusted him completely since the day I met him and not asked questions because I don't want to look like a nag and risk losing him.

The truth is, I know that he's too good for me. I'm punching well above my weight.

He's gorgeous, I mean head-turning, film-star gorgeous. He's tall and muscular with perfect teeth and a smile that turns knees weak. He should really be in the movies or on the TV, he's *that* stunning. Mum says that *he talks funny*, and she's not wrong; he doesn't talk like we do around here. I wonder if he tones his accent down for my benefit and to fit in because sometimes, he sounds like the posh people off the TV.

I don't want to doubt him because these last two months have been fantastic and I'm the happiest that I've ever been in my entire life.

I just wish he'd come home.

I count to sixty in my head and then throw back the duvet and force myself to jump out of bed and run to the bathroom. I lean over the bath and turn the shower taps to full and stand shivering as the water slowly runs hot. I quickly step out of my PJ's, pull my socks off and step into the bath and pull the plastic curtain across and stand underneath the hot water.

No point in moping around, it's time to get on with things.

* * *

The number seven bus into town picks up from the bus stop right outside Mum's block of flats so I wait until the last possible minute to leave my flat to catch it. Knowing my luck, she'll just happen to be looking out of the window and will be down the stairs and out to the bus stop if she sees me waiting there. I definitely can't tolerate her at the moment, especially as she has the uncanny knack of guessing when there's something bothering me.

I nearly leave it too late and have to sprint the last few metres to make sure the bus doesn't sail by without me. I pay my fare and sit on the single seat right at the front so that no one can sit next to me. I have my mask on and my hair down so even if anyone I know does get on, I'm hoping they won't notice it's me.

On the journey into town I mentally plan my route; I'll get off the bus and go straight round to the *Boots* in the precinct because it's the largest chemist and the busiest. I can pick up a pregnancy test with a bottle of shampoo or something and pay for it at the self-checkout so there'll be less chance of anyone I know seeing me and seeing what I'm buying.

Over the top?

Probably. But that's what comes of being paranoid about anyone else knowing too much about my life. When you've been dragged up by an alcoholic mother who can't keep her gob shut about anything you learn to be secretive.

I spend the rest of the bus journey catching up with Katrina's posts. Today she's going to the West End for lunch with the girls and to do some clothes shopping. There's a selfie of her in the back of a black cab with a cartoon picture of a champagne bottle and lots of shopping bags next to it. No doubt there'll be countless posts later on of all the fabulous meals she's going to eat with her friends. I've noticed that she rarely has her friends in her posts and when she does it's the back of their heads or they're blurred into the background. I'd hazard a guess that Katarina likes the limelight firmly on herself.

She's wearing a cream *Burberry* cotton trench coat and black *Gucci* sunglasses even though it's March and it's not at all sunny. I know all the brands of clothing and can spot them a mile away but if I didn't know, Katarina's feed tells me because she hashtags every single thing that she wears. Maybe she gets a discount from the companies or maybe she just likes showing off.

I have a pair of fake *Gucci's* that I got for ten pounds. They don't look any different from the ones she's wearing but I'd still like the real thing because who wants cheap fakes? I'm not a fan of *Burberry* but I'd still like the trench coat because it costs nearly seventeen-hundred-pounds.

Imagine having so much money that you could spend seventeen-hundred-pounds on a coat?

Imagine even *having* seventeen-hundred-pounds.

I flick her feed away and slip my phone into my pocket and wonder why life is so unfair. Why are some people born to have it all and others have nothing? I'm aware as I think this that I'm justifying stealing from her and I wait for a pang of guilt but it isn't forthcoming.

Usually when I come into town, I like to have a look around and do a bit of window shopping; today I could actually treat myself to something nice because I've managed to save up a couple of hundred pounds from the money Mac's been giving me. But I won't bother looking for anything because I'm not in the mood.

I have to plan what I'm going to do if the test confirms my suspicion that I'm pregnant. I'll have to make an appointment at the doctors and ask for the abortion pill or whatever it is or maybe I can buy it over the counter in *Boots*. I can only be a few weeks pregnant so it won't be a problem.

I won't tell Mac.

Because he's not going to want to be a father so what would be the point? There's no point at all.

And yet.

A tiny part of me wishes that I wasn't secretly going into town to buy a pregnancy test so I could secretly get the abortion pill if I am pregnant. A part of me wishes that Mac and I were a couple who'd known each other for a lot longer and could talk about it and decide what to do together.

Because I've spent my whole life being on my own and looking after myself, even though Mum has always been around, I've always felt alone and as if I was the one who was the adult.

Just for once I'd like to be looked after.

But it's too soon; Mac and I have only known each other for a couple of months, it's too much to put on him and from what he's said, he's *never* planning to having children.

That's if he comes back, of course, because I still haven't heard a word from him.

As this thought goes through my mind my phone bleeps and I quickly pull it out of my pocket. The disappointment is immediate; it's Mum. I don't open the message but slip my phone back into my pocket.

The bus pulls into the station and I get off and set off at a brisk pace towards the precinct. I'll get the test and then get the bus straight home; I'm in no mood to hang around. My phone bleeps twice in rapid succession and I pull it out of my pocket and glance at the screen to see that it's Mum again. She does this all the time; if I don't answer her immediately she'll blow up my phone for the rest of the day. I tap the icon and read the messages:

I need to talk to u

Can you come ova tonite

Why arnt u ansering

I wince at the bad spelling and quickly type a reply:

Am out for the day, will catch up with you

tomorrow xx

Seconds later she replies:

Were are u

In London for the day with Mac I reply, *going in to see a show in a minute so no signal. Will see you tomorrow xx*

She replies again but I don't open the message and slip my phone into my pocket. I hear it bleep twice more but ignore it; she'll get the message when I don't reply.

I push through the swing doors into *Boots* and head straight down the shop, scanning the area for anyone that I might know as I go. The shop is quiet and I grab two pregnancy tests and a bottle of shampoo and head for the self-service tills. Better to have two tests in case one is defective.

I pay for my shopping and in no time at all I'm out of the shop and heading back to the bus station. Another reason not to hang around in town is that Mum might be on one of her shoplifting visits and I definitely don't want to bump into her when I've told her that I'm in London.

I jump on the number seven just as the driver closes the doors and heave a sigh of relief.

Mission accomplished.

* * *

I get off the bus a stop early to avoid getting off at the bus stop opposite Mum's block of flats. I make my way back to my flat weaving through the back alleys just in case she's out and about. It takes me far longer than normal this way but I haven't exactly got much else to do. I scan the car park in front of my block of flats but there's no sign of Mac's car and I curse myself for getting my hopes up. I push through the door into my block and walk up to the flights of stairs to my flat. By the time I get inside I'm relieved I haven't bumped into anyone because I don't think I could stand having to talk because I feel so sorry for myself. I flop down onto the sofa and take one of the tests out of the carrier bag and slowly read the instructions.

It seems straightforward and there's no time like the present; I might as well get it over with and find out for sure. I stand up to go to the bathroom when I hear the unmistakable sound of the key in the front door. I quickly stuff the test back into the carrier bag and shove it behind a sofa cushion.

Mac's home.

CHAPTER SEVEN

'Mac,' I blurt out as he walks into the lounge. 'I thought you weren't coming back.'

'What?' He stops in his tracks and gives me a puzzled look. 'Why would you think that?' He cocks his head to one side and smiles that lazy smile and I feel like a fool; a stupid *needy* fool.

'You haven't messaged or anything, I was worried,' I say, lamely, wishing that I'd kept my mouth shut.

'I don't normally though, do I? he says, dropping his holdall onto the floor and walking across the room to me. 'You know it's difficult when I'm working. And it was worse this time because I had to get a new battery for my phone. This one kept playing up and I missed loads of messages.'

He circles his arms around my waist and pulls me close.

'Have you missed me, then?' he whispers, nuzzling my neck.

I hold him tightly, so pleased that he's back although I can't help a flash of annoyance; he could have used someone else's phone to message me, couldn't he?

'I always miss you,' I whisper.

'Good,' he says, slipping his hand underneath my sweatshirt. 'Because now you have to show me how much.'

* * *

'Seriously though, I *was* worried, Mac,' I say, as we lie snuggled up in bed, the room growing darker as the sun goes down outside.

'Why? There's no need to worry about me.'

'But what if you'd had an accident? I wouldn't even know, would I? I don't know your address or anything. You could be lying in a coma in hospital or something and I'd have no idea.'

'You don't need to know my address; I never stay there so there'd be absolutely no point,' Mac says. 'And of course you'd know if I'd had an accident, you're on my phone as my ICE contact.'

'ICE?' I ask.

'In case of emergency. Haven't you got me as yours?' he asks.

'No.' I have no idea what it even is. 'What is it?'

'Instead of putting me under Mac, you list me in your contacts as ICE, that way if I was in an accident whoever found me would know who to call.'

'Oh, I see. I don't have anyone on my phone as an ICE.'

'You should,' he says. 'Because how would I know if *you* were in an accident or taken ill? I can't see your mother bothering her arse to tell me.'

'Of course she'd tell you,' I say, feeling ridiculously pleased that he has me as his emergency contact. That must mean something, mustn't it?

'She wouldn't. She hates me for some reason, I can tell by the way she scowls at me.'

'She doesn't hate you,' I say. She does.

'She does. Not that I care one bit; it's you I want, not her. When I look at her I can't believe that she's your mother because you're nothing like each other, in looks or personality. You must have inherited your father's genes because you certainly didn't get any of hers. Thank Christ. Anyway, parents are over-rated and we don't need them when we're adults. Who needs whiney old people dragging us down and leeching off our youth and cramping our style? We should be like birds and kick offspring out of the nest as soon as they can fly and let them fend for themselves and leave them alone.'

I wince inwardly; I feel disloyal because I don't even attempt to stand up for Mum. Not that she deserves loyalty because she's never shown me any at all and he's right; she does hate him although I don't know why. You think she'd be pleased that I've met someone decent instead of the wasters who live around here. Although Mum is an inverted snob; she dislikes anyone who doesn't come from this estate and doesn't speak with a local accent.

Mac's words also kill stone dead any lingering secret hope that he'd be okay about me being pregnant. Thank God I hid the pregnancy tests before he came in, I need to get them from behind the sofa cushion and put them somewhere he's never going to find them as soon as possible.

Mac stretches his arms above his head and yawns loudly.

'I suppose we should get up because it's too early to go to bed, yet. And I'm hungry. I'm going to have a quick shower and then we should order in some food.' He throws the duvet back and climbs out of bed and saunters across the bedroom towards the wardrobe. I admire his muscular torso and toned arms and legs and marvel at the fact that he has the sort of skin that looks as if he has a permanent light tan, even his buttocks look tanned. He opens the wardrobe door and stares at the interior for a moment and then pulls out a shirt and a pair of jeans. He turns to the chest of drawers, yanks the bottom drawer open and pulls a pair of underpants out. He tucks all the clothes underneath one arm and heads towards the bathroom. The clothes he wore yesterday are scattered around the floor of the bedroom where he left them when he took them off.

As soon as I hear the bathroom door close, I leap

out of bed and wrap my dressing gown around me. I poke my head around the bedroom doorway to make sure he's in the bathroom and then hurry down the hallway to the lounge. I cross to the sofa and quickly pull the carrier bag from behind the cushion and hurry back to the bedroom. I take the pregnancy tests out of the bag and pull open the top drawer of the chest of drawers and bury both of the tests underneath my underwear.

There, done. There's no way Mac will look in there so they'll be quite safe until I have to use them. Which I won't be doing until he's gone away again because if they're positive – which I think they will be – I won't be able to hide my feelings from him. Better to find out while he's away and when he comes back it'll all be over and I'll no longer be pregnant.

I feel sick when I actually think the words but I put them out of my mind. What is wrong with me? It's not as if I even *want* a baby.

Absolutely no point in thinking about it now.

I'll just pretend it's not happening.

* * *

Mac sits back on the sofa and rubs his stomach.

'That,' he says. 'Was epic.'

I laugh and agree; we went for Thai tonight and it was great, much better than the Chinese we normally go for. We mostly order takeaways or go out for food when Mac's here; I'm not the greatest cook although I can cook a decent Chilli Con Carne and Lasagne, we can't have that all of the time. It doesn't help that my oven is temperamental; sometimes it just decides that it's going to not heat up properly and stuff that's been in there for hours comes out practically raw while at other times it incinerates stuff in minutes. There's no way that I can afford to buy another cooker so I just have to put up with it, which is why I mostly live on pasta and soup when I'm on my own.

I wonder if I'll ever have enough money to have a decent cooker instead of someone's old cast-off. I'd like to try cooking different recipes instead of the diet of takeaways and bread and margarine that I was brought up on.

Katarina has a state of the art kitchen but she never posts pictures of any food that she's cooked, just arty pictures of frothy coffees from her fancy coffee machine. They probably eat out all of the time because somehow, I can't see her peeling potatoes or chopping onions, or even getting her hands dirty.

'You're deep in thought.' Mac is leaning back against the sofa studying me. 'Why so serious?'

I laugh. No way am I going to tell him what I'm thinking, I don't want him to think I'm a complete nut job who's obsessed with her lookalike's *Instagram*.

'I was just thinking about when you were away,' I lie. 'When I didn't hear from you I was afraid you might have got caught breaking into Katarina's house.'

He frowns and I can tell that I've annoyed him.

'For Christ's sake, Jess, what do you take me for? I'm not some sort of amateur, you know.'

I shrug. 'Well, you did ask what I was thinking.'

He's silent for a moment and then gets up from the sofa and crosses to his giant holdall that's been lying in the middle of the lounge since he arrived. I know that unless I move it, it'll stay exactly where he dropped it until he leaves again. He unzips it and pulls out a large brown envelope and returns to the sofa and sits down.

He opens the flap of the envelope and looks at me and smiles.

'Want to see?' he teases.

'Yes please,' I say, having no idea what he's about to show me.

He puts his fingers inside the envelope and pulls out a blue book which I quickly realise is a passport.

'Have a look,' he says, offering it to me.

I open the passport and for a moment I think that it's my own; and then I realise that it's Katarina's.

'You stole her passport?' I gasp.

'Of course not,' he snorts. 'It's not real, it's a clone.'

I leaf through the pages. I'm no expert on passports and the only one that I've ever seen is my own but it looks, and feels, real.

'It's so real,' I say. 'I can't believe it's not real.'

'Well, it is real, for what we need,' Mac says. 'And the only way it would be found out is if we actually tried to use it at the airport because the biometric chip is fake. And as we're never going to be doing that it's not a problem.'

'It even has the pages stamped,' I say.

'Like I say, it's an exact copy. She'd struggle to tell the difference herself.'

'It's amazing. Who did it?' I ask. 'And how did you get hers to copy?' He doesn't answer but takes the passport from my hand and drops it back into the envelope and then pulls out a bank card and hands it to me. I stare at the card with Katarina's name on it and slowly turn it over and examine it.

'It's so real.'

'Yeah,' Mac says. 'The contact I use is the best – and the most expensive, but you get what you pay for. And he's fast; it only took him two days.'

'But how did you get hold of her passport and card to copy?'

Mac laughs harshly and he has a strange expression on his face and for a moment I feel almost afraid of him.

'Some people are so stupid,' he says. 'And *way* too trusting. I only had to watch her house for a few days and I knew her routine like the back of my hand.'

He looks at me and I see that he's pleased with himself and wants me to ask; he wants to impress me.

'You did?'

'Yeah. The husband's out of the house from seven in the morning 'til eight in the evening and she must be a bit thick because she doesn't even lock the back door when she's at home. In London. Unbelievable. Talk about stupid. It's a big house and two of you could live in there and not see each other for a week if you wanted it that way. All I had to do was wait for the chance and slip in the back door when she wasn't looking.'

'What, you went in while she was there?' I feel my heart start to race. 'What if she'd caught you?'

'Wouldn't have been a problem,' Mac says. 'Although it would have scuppered our plans.' He laughs that weird laugh again, and this time I *am* afraid of him.

'Anyway, she didn't catch me because like most people, she's completely predictable. I found her passport in a drawer in the study along with all of her passwords in a notebook. It's incredible how stupid some people are. The bank card I took from her handbag that she leaves on a table in the hallway. It didn't take long to photograph it all and then I put it back. She didn't even know I'd been in there.'

I sit silently and try to imagine myself doing something like that; I know I wouldn't have the nerve to even try.

'Talk about thick as shit; they have a fancy, expensive alarm and she can't even lock the back door. She probably thinks because she has a garden at the back of the house it offers some sort of protection. It's actually quite the opposite; a garden is a godsend to any thief worth his salt because that's the easiest route into a mark's house.'

'You're amazing, I say, not really sure if I mean it.

'I am,' he says, smiling.

'What happens now?' I ask. 'What are you going to do with the passport and card?'

'I'm not going to do anything with it,' he says. 'You are.'

'Me? What can I do?'

'You're going to impersonate Katarina Hepworth-Jones,' he says, quietly.

'Am I?' My mouth has suddenly gone dry.

'You are.'

'How? I mean, what am I going to do?'

'You're going to open a bank account in her name, and you're going to use the passport and the bank card to do it.'

I stare at him and it hits me.

We're really doing this.

CHAPTER EIGHT

We didn't talk any more about opening the bank account last night because we got carried away planning what we're going to do in our new life in Spain. I asked Mac if we'd need to get jobs and he laughed and said no, but maybe we could open a bar of our own or something later on after we've had a good rest. It took my breath away when he said it because how much money does he think we're going to have?

I felt sick as well actually, because I'm scared to death and I don't know if I can do it. It's all very well talking about it but have I actually got the guts to see it through? Mum might be an accomplished shop-lifter but apart from a school library book I've never stolen anything in my life. The thought of going into a bank and opening a bank account whilst pretending to be someone else fills me with fear. What if I mess it up and get caught? What if I end up going to prison?

I wait until we've finished breakfast – toast for me, last night's takeaway leftovers for Mac – before I broach the subject.

'I've been thinking about the bank account thing. Why don't we open it online?' I ask. 'I think you can upload your ID and verify it online too. It'll be safer than actually going into a bank in person.'

Mac doesn't speak for a moment and then he abruptly gets up from the table and walks across to the sink and stares out of the window.

'I knew it,' he says, turning around to face me, his arms folded. 'You've got cold feet, haven't you?'

I stare up at him, not knowing what to say.

'I thought you were too quiet about it last night,' he goes on. 'You should have told me you weren't up for it before I went ahead and had the stuff cloned. I wouldn't have gone to all this trouble and spent a shitload of money.'

'I have got the guts,' I lie. 'But surely it'll be safer to do it online?'

'You can't do it online,' he says, very slowly as if I'm not understanding what he's saying. 'Because you have to deposit some money to open the account and how can you do that online?'

'I could use her debit card?' I suggest.

'And what will happen when you use that card?'

I look at him blankly, aware that I've failed some sort of test.

'If you use the card, she'll see the transaction on her statement and she'll know that she didn't make it and that someone else did. She'll contact her bank and cancel the debit card. She'll be alerted to the fact that we've cloned it and it'll be over; end of plan. I thought you understood; we're not going to use her card before we need to otherwise it's not going to work.'

'You haven't told me the plan,' I say.

'There's no point if you're backing out. I thought you wanted out of this shithole of a country; I thought you wanted a new life in Spain.' He almost shouts at me.

'I do want a new life and I'm not backing out,' I say. 'I just thought it would be safer doing it online. I didn't realise about the deposit. Honestly, Mac, I *want* to do this.'

'Okay,' he says, in a softer tone, sitting down at the table. 'I'm sorry I haven't explained everything to you but it's better if you don't know until we come to do it. You don't want to walk into that bank and your face give away everything we have planned. You have to *believe* you're just opening a bank account and nothing more. You just have to convince yourself that you're Katarina for a few hours and everything will fall into place. I'll give you some cash to open the account and it'll be easy; you'll be in and out of there in no time.'

I nod as if I agree but inside I feel sick.

I don't think I can do it but I can't tell him that.

'So we're good, yeah?' Mac reaches across the table and takes hold of my hand. He looks deep into my eyes.

'Yes,' I say. We're good.'

'That's my girl.'

'When do I need to do this?' I ask.

'You're still following her on *Instagram*?' he asks, not answering my question.

'I am,' I say, happy to be talking about something I'm comfortable with. 'I check her account every few hours. I feel like I know her.' I laugh but it's true, I do. I pick my phone up and open up the app. This morning she's *chilling with a good book,* there's a picture of a thick hardback book held open halfway through, the sleeve of her sweatshirt and watch displayed to good effect. If I didn't already know what brand they were she's hash tagged the watch and the sweatshirt. The sweatshirt is *Alexander Wang* and I feel a flash of hatred for her that she's able to spend a couple of hundred pounds on something to wear just to slob around at home. I wonder if she's even reading the book or if she's just posed with it because it's top of the bestseller lists.

'Anything interesting?' Mac asks.

'Not yet,' I say, scrolling down her account. It's barely eleven o'clock and she's already posted loads of photos.

'Hang on,' I say, clicking on a picture of a luxury hotel that she's posted.

Winter sun! She's written, *off for a well-earned two weeks in the Maldives.*

'She's going on holiday,' I say, as I continue to scroll.

Mac looks up with interest.

'When?'

'Hang on, let me see.' I scroll through pictures of expensive bikinis that she likes and a set of *Gucci* suitcases that she's tagged to buy until I reach the part that I need to know.

'A week tomorrow,' I say. 'There's even a picture of the hotel they're staying at.'

'Perfect,' Mac mutters. 'That works for us. It *so* works for us.' He grins.

I smile, although my mouth is so dry it feels as if my lips will stick to my teeth, I hold the phone screen in front of him so he can see her posts.

'What a stupid bitch,' Mac says. 'She might as well just put a sign up saying *come burgle me* by putting it all over social media.'

The thought crosses my mind that maybe someone *will* burgle her and then we won't have to go through with this.

Do I want that to happen?

No, I remind myself, I want a new life.

I have to do this.

'Going back to the bank account thing, Mac,' I say, in what I hope is a casual manner. 'What if the bank sends a letter to her house and she opens it? I mean, there'll be a new bank card and stuff and she'll see it, won't she?'

'No, she won't,' Mac smiles broadly. 'Because she won't be here, will she? She'll be in the Maldives. The bank will take about a week to send out the paperwork and she'll be gone by then. And I'll be in her house to receive any post that comes through the door so it won't be a problem. By the time she comes back from her holiday we'll be long gone and it'll be too late for her to stop us.'

'Oh.'

'That's why we need to get moving. Tomorrow morning you need to get on a train to London and go and open that bank account. I've got a copy of one of her utility bills because you'll need that as well and I've picked a bank nearest the station so you don't need to hang about.'

'Where will you be? Can't you come with me?' I ask. 'Do you have to go back to work so soon? You've barely been here a day.'

'I've got stuff to do tomorrow,' he says. 'Things for our future. And I wouldn't come with you even if I could because banks have CCTV, don't they? I'll be back here tomorrow night and then I can stay for a few days.'

'Okay.'

'And before you know it,' he says, with a grin. 'We'll be on our way to a new life in the sun with a big wodge of cash and this shithole will be a dim and distant memory.'

I smile and try to believe him but I can't imagine it; I want to, but I can't.

'I know you're nervous,' he says, reading my mind. 'But you've got to have faith.'

I nod and smile but my mouth is dry and I feel sick.

I have to have faith.

I have to *believe*.

* * *

I'm going to cook us some dinner tonight, just steak and oven chips but it'll make a change from takeaways. I'm going to the Asda on the far end of the estate and then I'll call in and see Mum on the way back. I don't want to see her but she'll only turn up here if I don't.

Mac is on his phone when I walk into the lounge and as his fingers fly over the screen, I wonder who he's texting. He says he's tired after the last few days and I think maybe the strain is getting to him just like it's getting to me but there's no way he'll admit it.

'Sure you don't want to come?' I ask, slipping my jacket on.

'What, on your exciting trip to Asda?' He grins. 'No, you're alright, I'm going to stay here and chill. Might even have a nap in front of the TV.'

I knew he wouldn't come, which is just as well because if he had I couldn't go to Mum's.

'Okay, well I won't be too long although I might call in at Mum's on the way back.'

'Great,' he says, pulling a face. 'What a shame I'm not coming.'

'She's not that bad,' I say.

Mac makes a snorting sound and I laugh.

'Give her my love,' he says. 'And her lovely beau, Seamus.'

'Stop it.' I giggle as I lean over the sofa and kiss

him.

I go out to the hallway and put my jacket on and zip it up and let myself out of the door. As I head down the flights of stairs, I try to imagine a new life in the sun. I have to keep reminding myself that if I want it, I'm going to have to earn it by doing what Mac says; opening that bank account.

How hard can it be?

I'll find out tomorrow.

I push open the door of the stairwell into the entrance of the block and stride through the main doors and out into a blustery day that nearly knocks me off my feet. I put my head down and tuck my hands into my pockets which is when I realise that I don't have my purse.

Sod it.

That means I'll have to go all the way back up the stairs and get it.

I about turn and walk straight back in and make my way up the stairs. This is what happens when I have a lot on my mind, I forget the basics like taking my purse out with me.

I let myself in the front door and quickly walk down the hallway and into the lounge, narrowly avoiding falling over Mac's holdall in the process. Mac is so very nearly the perfect man but his untidiness is unbelievable; he must be the messiest person in the world and simply drops stuff where he stands and leaves it there. I'm naturally tidy and at first, I didn't pick up after him as I thought it might irritate him but he's completely oblivious. He has no idea how his dirty clothes get from the floor to the washing machine and then back in the wardrobe; he must think it happens by magic. I grab the handles of the holdall and drag it to the side of the room, out of the way.

I'm surprised to see that Mac's no longer on the sofa. Maybe he's so tired that he's gone to bed. I spot my purse amongst Mac's clutter that's already accumulated on the coffee table and I pick it up and slip it in my pocket. I go back out into the hall, walking quietly so that I don't disturb him if he's trying to sleep.

The bedroom door is shut as I walk by and I'm surprised to hear the sound of Mac talking; he must be on his mobile. I stand still for a moment outside the door and listen but I can't make out what he's saying, only that he's speaking quickly. The floorboard that I'm standing on makes a sudden creaking sound and I feel instantly guilty; what if he came out and caught me listening? How embarrassing would that be?

I tiptoe down the hallway and let myself out into the corridor and quickly walk along to the stairwell and head down the stairs.

I feel a bit bad for *almost* eavesdropping; I wasn't doing it deliberately because it's not something that I'd consciously do, it just sort of happened.

As I walk down the stairs there's something niggling at the back of my mind but I can't grasp what it is. I have the feeling that there's something I'm missing but have no idea what. Is it because he's making a phone call? I'm over thinking things as usual because he's allowed to make a phone call and there's nothing wrong with that, is there? It's not as if he's doing anything wrong and it's not as if he went into the bedroom to do it secretly because I wasn't even there. I give myself a mental shake, I'm getting as bad as Mum.

I trust Mac completely.

Don't I?

CHAPTER NINE

I search the shelves in Asda for the best looking piece of steak and wonder why I don't know anything about buying meat, how do people learn these things? Is it something their mothers teach them? If it is then I've no hope; all Mum has ever taught me is that it's fine to steal as long as you don't get caught.

And as it turns out I'm no better than her, am I, because she steals from shops whereas I'm going to steal from an actual person, so I'm probably worse.

I force my train of thought back to the steak, because the middle of the Asda meat aisle is definitely not the place to start questioning my life choices.

So, which is best, fillet or rump? I honestly have no idea; Mac would know but I want to surprise him by cooking for him so I couldn't actually ask him. I pull out my phone and do a quick internet search to find out. Ten minutes later I'm totally confused as to which one to buy as there are so many differing opinions. I decide to go for the most expensive and hope for the best.

Before I put my phone away, I quickly check Katarina's *Instagram*; I tell myself that it's because Mac wants me to keep up to date with what she's doing but, in all honesty, I feel compelled to find out what she's posted since I last looked. I scroll past photos of her lunch – mango salad with avocado bursts, whatever they are – to a picture of a long black velvet dress – hashtag *Ralph Lauren*, draped elegantly across the neatly-made bed with the caption *who's going out to dinner tonight?* I feel suddenly pathetic for agonising over buying a piece of steak from Asda. Is that really going to impress Mac, is he going to be thrilled that I'm cooking him steak and oven chips?

I don't think so.

I click off my phone with a sigh and stuff it back into my jacket pocket and stare at the shelf of steak. Any enthusiasm I had for cooking tonight is now gone and I'm seriously considering not bothering and just ordering a takeaway as usual when I hear a familiar voice behind me.

'Hiya, mate. Long time no see.'

I turn around to see my friend Dani standing right behind me.

'Hi, Dani.' I grin, giving her a hug. 'It's been ages! How are you?' It is ages; the last time I saw her was the night we went out clubbing together and I met Mac. That was over two months ago;

I feel my cheeks flush pink with guilt that I haven't bothered contacting her and then remind myself that she hasn't contacted *me*, either, so I've absolutely no need to feel bad.

'I'm good, how about you?' she asks. 'What you been up to? You still with that hot guy you copped off with at *Vadims*?'

'Yeah, I am,' I say, surprised that she's remembered. She was so wasted by the time I met Mac that she could barely stand up. She'd spent most of the night slumped in one of the booths with her on/off boyfriend Jake because she'd pre-loaded on practically a whole bottle of vodka before we even got out of my flat. Her binge drinking's one of the reasons I don't go out with her very often. I can't keep up and I always end up going home on my own because Jake always makes a bee-line for her when she's pissed.

'That's a long time for you,' Dani says. 'You usually go full psycho on them after a couple of weeks. He must be behaving himself.'

'How about you?' I ask, ignoring her comment. 'You and Jake still together?'

'Nah,' she waves her hand. 'Had enough of him, we're done.'

I look at her and laugh and she joins in after a moment. She says this all the time and the following week they're back together.

'Well, for this week anyway. When are you going to let us meet your fella, then?' she asks. 'What's his name?'

'Mac,' I say. 'And it's a bit difficult arranging stuff because he works away a lot.'

'When he's here we should all go out together one night, make an effort to meet up,' Dani suggests. 'I know Taylor's got a new bloke and I don't mind being gooseberry if me and Jake aren't together. I can get my mum to mind Cherise.'

'Yeah, sounds like a great idea,' I say, having absolutely no intention of doing it. 'I'll find out his dates for working and sort something for when he's back.'

'Yeah,' Dani says, slowly. 'You should do that. 'Cos I know you've been out and about with him 'cos some of my mates have seen you with him. He's a bit posh, isn't he? You worried we'll show you up?'

There's an edge to her voice when she says it and I wonder who's seen me and Mac when we've gone up town. It could be anyone; you can't sneeze around here without someone asking if you've got a cold.

'Course not,' I say. 'And he's not posh at all, where did you get that idea from?'

She shrugs. 'I dunno, might have been your mum, I can't remember.'

This is why I hate Mum knowing anything about my life, she just cannot keep her mouth shut.

'Well, you don't want to listen to anything she says,' I say. 'You know she never lets the truth get in the way of a good story.'

Dani looks at me blankly as if she doesn't get what I said and I remember that she's not the brightest; if she was she wouldn't keep going back to the same waste of space boyfriend who keeps cheating on her.

'So anyway,' I say, edging away from her. 'I've got to go now but text me some dates and we'll sort a night out, yeah?'

'Okay,' she says, slowly, giving me a strange look. 'See ya.'

I put my hand up in a half-wave and turn and walk quickly down the aisle and turn into the next one. Forget the steak, we'll get a takeaway. I don't want to go out on a night out with her or Taylor or anyone else from around here. I know instinctively that Mac won't like my friends and he especially won't like Jake and will make no attempt to hide it.

I'm basically giving up my friends for a man, so what does that say about me?

It says that I'm just like Dani and Taylor; because it's exactly what they've always done.

* * *

When I knock on the door to Mum's flat, I can hear her talking so I guess that Seamus is in. The walls are thin on these flats and Mum also has only one volume, which is extra loud, so if I stood here long enough I could listen to every single word she's saying. I won't though, because Mum has no secrets and by association nor does anyone who knows her because she broadcasts *everything* so I wouldn't be finding out anything that the entire town doesn't already know.

I wish I'd thought to listen before I knocked to check whether Seamus was in but it's too late now, I've committed myself. I'll have to go in and see her and Seamus, who gives me the creeps.

When mum opens the door, I jump back in mock fright and scream; she has a plastic highlighting cap on her head with strands of bleach smothered hair pulled through the holes.

'Christ,' I shout. 'I thought I'd come to the zombie house.'

'Ha, ha, very funny,' Mum says, without laughing as she steps aside to let me in.

'I thought you only had it done a couple of weeks ago,' I say, as I walk down the hallway to the kitchen.

'No, it was ages ago,' she says, as she follows behind. 'I like to keep the colour fresh.'

It wasn't ages ago, it was definitely a couple of weeks but I don't argue because it's pointless, Mum will never admit that she's wrong even when the truth is staring her in the face. She has Seamus bleach it for her so often that her whole head is white blonde, rather than highlighted. I'm surprised her hair hasn't fallen out with the amount of dye it's had on it over the years.

I walk into the kitchen and Seamus is sitting at the table rolling up a joint. He looks up and grunts something at me that I don't catch but I assume is *hello.*

'Hi,' I say. I walk over to the sink, turn around and lean against it and cross my arms. I have no intention of sitting anywhere near him.

'You can sit down, you know,' Mum says, as she comes into the kitchen and plonks herself down in the chair opposite Seamus.

'I will in a minute,' I lie.

I don't want to be that close to Seamus.

Seamus finishes rolling his joint and places it between his rubbery lips and lights it. He sucks deeply on it and then offers it to Mum but she shakes her head and pulls a cigarette out of the packet lying on the table and lights it up. I'm going to stink of cigarette smoke and weed when I leave here and I can already imagine Mac wrinkling his nose when he gets close to me.

There's a small leather pouch in front of Seamus on the table and he starts to pull stuff out of it and line it up in a neat line on the table in front of him. Tiny plastic bags of coke, twists of weed and small bottles of clear liquid, the bag is stuffed full. Seamus points to each item and counts it, mouthing the numbers as he goes.

'Seamus just likes to help his friends out,' Mum says, seeing me watching. 'He's not a dealer or nothing.'

I don't say anything; she trots the same lie out every time, although I don't know why she feels the need to justify what he does; he's hardly unusual on this estate. There's a dealer around every street corner.

'Sort you something?' Seamus looks up and asks me with a leer.

'No, I'm alright, thanks.' I say, without emotion. I know he's only trying to get a reaction out of me.

'I've told you before, our Jess don't do drugs,' Mum says, proudly. 'She don't even smoke fags.'

She has no idea; she thinks she knows me so well. Of course I've tried drugs because around here it would be impossible not to. There was a time when Dani, Taylor and I used to go out clubbing at the weekends with a supply of cocaine to take us through the night but it was a phase that didn't last long. I couldn't really afford it – although it's cheaper than buying the booze in the clubs – but the main reason was that I've seen too many of my old school mates progress from cocaine to the harder stuff and it never ends well. And it made my nose sore.

'Bit of GHB?' Seamus picks up one of the little bottles and wiggles it at me. 'I'll let you have the first one free as a taster, see if you like it.'

'Why would I want that?' I ask, deadpan. 'I'm not planning on raping anyone.'

'It's not just for that,' Seamus rolls his eyes. 'Christ, you're such an innocent. You get a nice high from it if you use it right.'

'No, you're alright,' I say.

'You sure?' Seamus wiggles his eyebrows and winks at me. 'It can spice things up in the bedroom if you get my drift. You and your posh bloke could try it out. It's good ain't it, Sal? Works for us.'

Mum giggles and I stay silent. I want to gag at the thought of it. No way do I want to hear anything about their sex life or how they spice it up, it's just revolting. I wish I hadn't come here now and I wonder why I bothered.

And then I remember; I'm *never* coming back here once Mac and I go to Spain so I won't have to do it for much longer.

I look at Mum and try to imagine missing her.

I can't.

It'll just be a relief that I don't have to come round here anymore; the only reason I visit is to stop her coming to my flat and staying all day winding me up.

'How's *he* then?' Mum asks between drags. 'About, is he?'

'Do you mean Mac?' I ask.

'Well unless you've got another bloke on the go, yeah, I mean him.' She sniggers and Seamus laughs with her as he stuffs the drugs back into the leather pouch, his tongue clamped between his teeth. God, he's thick. And revolting.

'He's fine,' I say.

'*Fine*,' Mum mimics. 'Bloody hell, you're even starting to talk like him. I'm surprised you can lower yourself to come round here and see me.'

'Come on then, spit it out, Mum,' I say, knowing that there's something she wants to get off her chest. 'What's your problem now?'

'I aint' got a problem,' she says, stubbing out

her cigarette in the overflowing ashtray before immediately lighting another. '*He's* the problem. You're too trusting. I tried to tell you, he ain't what you think he is, he's a crook and he's no better than anyone else around here even though he talks posh.'

'Oh, for fuck's sake,' I say, exasperated with her. 'Not this again. He isn't posh and he's not a crook so give it a rest.'

'Well, that's a nice way to talk to your mother,' Mum says, indignantly. 'I'm only looking out for you.'

'No, you're not,' I say, walking towards the door. 'You're just poking your nose in and looking for something to gossip about like you always do and I'm not staying here to listen to it.'

'You'll wish you had.' I hear Mum call out as I walk down the hallway. I should just tell her that I know exactly what Mac is and what we have planned and that would stop her slagging him off. She'd be super impressed but she can't keep her mouth shut and will have broadcast it all around the estate by this afternoon, so I daren't say a word. And I don't want her knowing I'm going to Spain because she's definitely not getting an invite to visit. Although I doubt she'd come because she doesn't even have a passport and there's not much chance of her getting one because you can't shoplift one.

'Don't come crying to me when it all goes tits up,' she shouts from the kitchen and I hear Seamus laughing in his peculiar braying donkey way.

'No chance,' I bellow, as I yank open the front door. 'And I'd rinse that bleach off if I was you before your hair falls out.'

Mum doesn't answer but I hear the screech of chair legs on lino as she pushes it back and gets up from the table.

I storm down the corridor and open the door to the stairwell and run down the stairs. I wonder why I let her get to me so much and then remember that it won't be for much longer.

I won't miss her one little bit.

CHAPTER TEN

I'm so nervous about the bank visit that I didn't think I'd sleep at all last night but amazingly, I did. If I believed in omens, which I usually don't, I'd believe that luck was on my side today because when I awoke, I felt the familiar dull ache in the pit of my stomach that told me that my period had arrived.

I jumped out of bed and left Mac still sound asleep and by the time I got to the bathroom my knickers were sodden. I felt such relief but also something else.

A little bit disappointed.

Completely stupid, I know, because no way am I in any position to have a baby. I think that maybe the false alarm made me realise that actually, one day in the future I *would* like a baby and I felt disappointment because I know that will be impossible with Mac. He's made his feelings clear on the subject of children; he doesn't ever want any because they tie you down and suck the life out of you. I know people change their minds but I don't think Mac will because he sounded like he hated the thought of children and of being a parent.

So I can have Mac or I can have children, not both.

I get into the shower and blast the stupid thoughts from my head. There's absolutely no point in thinking about it now.

I lather up the shampoo and take particular care in washing and conditioning my hair because today I have to look good.

Today I'm going to be Katarina.

I have to get it into my head that I'm her for the day if I'm going to pull this off. I have to *believe* that I'm her to be able to do it. I can't go into that bank as *Jess off the sink estate* otherwise they're going to be able to smell that I'm a fake from a mile off. I have to walk and talk and *feel* like Katarina.

After I've showered, I towel dry my hair, put my underwear on and slip my dressing gown on and go into the kitchen. There's still no sound from Mac so I guess he's still asleep. I put the kettle on and as I lean against the sink, waiting for it to boil, I flick through *Instagram* until I find Katarina's account.

She's posted several times already and it's only a quarter to nine. *Time to get beach ready!* she captions beneath a picture of a bright yellow bikini with matching flips-flops spread over her bed with a link to an upmarket tanning salon. The bed is unmade but it's fake unmade because it looks far too neat and tidy to be real. The luxurious, silk quilt is drawn back as if she's just tumbled out of bed but I zoom in and the bottom sheet is pristine, looking almost as if it's been ironed and the pillow is plumped and un-dented by her head. *Pre-holiday golden glow*, she gushes, *can't wait!*

Is her whole life as fake as her *Instagram* profile? Can she actually do anything that doesn't get posted to her account? Her entire life seems to be one long photo opportunity and it's all about *her*. Her husband rarely gets a mention; sometimes there'll be a photo of him but he's not photogenic or glamorous like her and she never actually mentions him in her comments. I scroll through her account until I find a post with him in it. He's overweight and older than her, older than I at first thought, nearer to fifty than forty or maybe even older. He dresses like an old man and looks a mess for someone with so much money. He obviously isn't obsessed with his looks like Katarina is with hers. In one post he's wearing what I assume to be a very expensive suit but it looks awful on him; the jacket is unbuttoned and the waistband of the trousers is tight and tucked underneath a rounded belly which is straining the buttons of his shirt. Ugh, he could easily be taken for her father. I assume she's only with him for his money so he can buy her everything she wants and he's with her because she's young and pretty and looks good on his arm.

She must be with him for his money because I can't see what else there is to attract her to him. Is that what you have to do to get the life you want, basically prostitute yourself to a man old enough to be your father? Is that any better than stealing, selling yourself?

Or maybe I'm just trying to justify my own actions. Does stealing trump prostitution? I think it does because she's only hurting herself by staying with him for his money whereas I'll be hurting someone else. I do know that I couldn't stay with some old man for his money; I couldn't do that to myself. I think of Mac and how we can't keep our hands off each other and how much I love him. I look back at the photo of her husband and shudder at the thought of having to have sex with him. I almost feel sorry for Katarina.

Unless she loves him, of course, because anything is possible. Mum says she loves Seamus and he's beyond revolting, so who knows?

Mac still hasn't told me exactly what we're stealing and how; but he'll have to tell me soon because once Katarina's away on holiday whatever it is, it's going to happen.

The kettle boils and I spoon coffee into two mugs; I'll have to wake Mac up soon because I have to dry my hair and the hairdryer is noisy and will wake him up anyway. I make the coffee and am about to take it into the bedroom when Mac saunters into the kitchen wearing just his underpants.

'Morning beautiful.' He crosses to me and wraps his arms around me and kisses my neck, giving my bottom a quick squeeze.

'Eww, bed breath,' I say, pushing him away with a laugh.

He laughs and picks up the coffee I've made him.

'I'll drink this in bed,' he says. 'You coming?'

'Yes,' I say, picking up my mug. 'But not back to bed, I have to dry my hair.'

We walk through the bedroom and Mac jumps back into bed and pats the space next to him.

'Come on,' he says. 'Just come back for a little while.'

'I can't,' I say. 'I have to get ready.'

'Spoilsport,' Mac says. 'Take your clothes off and do it naked, then, and I can watch.'

'No.' I laugh, although I do take my dressing gown off and stand there in my bra and knickers while I rummage around in the drawer for the hairdryer. 'I have to get in character and be Katarina today.'

'Maybe she does it for her husband,' Mac says. 'Naked hair drying.'

'I don't think so,' I say, with a snort. 'He's so old the excitement would probably kill him.'

I plug the hairdryer in and turn it on and carefully tease my hair into shape. When I've finished I survey the results with satisfaction; it looks just as good as when I left the salon. I wonder if there's anywhere around here where I can get it cut as well as Alun did it and then remind myself; I won't be here.

I put the hairdryer away and pull open the wardrobe doors and try and decide what I'm going to wear.

'Don't get dressed yet,' Mac says.

'Mac,' I say, turning and smiling at him. 'I have to get dressed, I'm going into London, remember?'

'I know,' he says, leaping out of bed. 'But none of your crappy clothes are good enough for Katarina.' He disappears through the doorway and I close the wardrobe doors and wait for him to come back. I know my clothes are cheap but I can't help feeling a bit hurt, they might not be designer but I like to think I always look as good as I can. I hear the sound of him unzipping his holdall and wonder what he has for me to wear; I hope he's not had it screwed up in there because that means I'll have to iron it and I want to get going and get this over and done with.

He returns holding a carrier bag in his hand and gives it to me. I open the bag and pull out a navy blue, silk jumpsuit. I hold it up and study it, it doesn't seem crumpled at all and I see by the label that it's *Jaeger.* I'm almost sure I've seen Katarina wear this.

Mac climbs back into bed and watches me with interest as I reach into the bag and pull out a mustard coloured military style jacket in soft cotton. I know now that Katarina has definitely posted this on *Instagram* and I put the jacket to my nose and sniff.

'What's the matter?' Mac asks. 'Does it smell?'

'It does,' I say, staring at him. 'It smells of perfume.'

Mac smirks.

'You took this from her house?' I ask, although I already know the answer.

He shrugs and I throw the jumpsuit and jacket onto the bed.

'I'll wear my own clothes,' I say, pulling open the wardrobe doors.

'But why?' Mac asks.

'I don't want to wear another woman's clothes.' I start pushing hangers along the rail, looking for something suitable.

Mac climbs out of bed and comes over and puts his hand over mine to stop me from moving the hangers.

'Look, I know you don't want to wear her clothes but you have to.' He circles his arm around my waist and pulls me towards him. 'You have to look the part. It's only for a few hours.'

'You stole them,' I say, stating the obvious. 'What if she notices?'

He laughs and releases his hold of me.

'Trust me, she won't. She has a roomful of wardrobes with so many clothes in them that she probably never wears the same outfit twice.'

I stare at him.

'Go on,' he urges. 'Just try them on and if you really don't like them you don't have to wear them.'

'Okay, then,' I sigh, walking over to the bed and

picking up the jumpsuit.

'But I really can't see that it's going to make any difference.'

* * *

As the train pulls into Paddington, I let all the other passengers get off before I attempt to stand up. I don't want to be crushed in the scrabble to get off the train. As I stand up, I check my reflection in the window; my hair looks great and I took extra care when applying my make up; just enough to look as if I've made an effort but not overdone, not cheap.

Under-stated and classy, Mac says.

He was right about the clothes; they just look so different but more than that, they *feel* different. Once I'd slipped the jumpsuit on I never wanted to take it off, the fabric felt soft and comfortable and didn't crease at all. I slipped the jacket on and marvelled at the cut of it; it could have been made for me.

Which I suppose it was, really.

I stood in front of the mirror and stared at myself and I felt as if I was looking at Katarina, I seemed to stand taller and hold myself differently. It was very strange.

You look so like her Mac had said huskily from his position stretched out on the bed, and then he said *he couldn't wait to rip her clothes off me when I got back.* I'd laughed and said no way was he ripping them off me because I was keeping them to wear again. He said *say that again like Katarina* and although I don't really know what she sounds like I repeated it, only more slowly, saying each word carefully. *Perfect* he'd growled, *we can celebrate tonight, Katarina.* I'd giggled but I knew we wouldn't be celebrating in our normal way but I didn't say anything. Why spoil the moment and tell him that I had rotten stomach ache because I'd just got my period.

Once I was ready Mac drove me to the station because he said women who wear clothes like that don't take buses. I felt relieved because I had a horrible feeling that I'd bump into someone I knew and I wanted to avoid that at all costs. I was also wearing a pair of heels that aren't the most comfortable. They're a cheap pair that I bought from *Primark* but they look okay as they're barely noticeable underneath the trousers. I have a fake *Gucci* handbag and even that looks okay next to the outfit. Mac said to ring him when I'm on the train coming back and he'll pick me up from the station.

On the way to the station, we went through the plan and what I was going to say and we've done this so many times that I wanted to scream. But I didn't of course, because I have to get this right because there is no second chance.

Whenever I feel the nerves get the better of me, I remind myself that I want to do this because I want a different life. I want to be able to wear clothes like this but I want the clothes to be mine, not stolen from someone else.

I have to do it.

Not least because if I don't, I know that I'll lose Mac because he won't be able to take it if I fail. He has such faith in me and I don't want to disappoint him. He's taken a lot of risks and spent a lot of money on fake documents to get me to this point; all I have to do is pretend to be someone else for a short while. I have the fake passport and debit card, a utility bill in her and her husband's name and three-hundred-pounds in cash to open the account. I even have a story if they ask; I need a savings account where I can put my earnings from being a social media influencer as I'm earning so much money now that I need to put it somewhere where it'll earn interest. I even have a reason for using cash; I never use anything but cards so want to get rid of the cash that I have. I'm to offer the card at first and then suddenly remember that I have wads of cash in my purse. I drew out cash as the builders who renovated my property liked to be paid in cash instalments but I drew out too much. This will save me going into my bank and depositing it, I'm to say.

But I mustn't make it sound like I've rehearsed it.

I'll be so glad when it's over.

I get off the train and cross the platform and make my way to the exit. As I walk briskly along, I go over the plan in my head one more time and in what seems like minutes I arrive at the bank.

I can't believe that I got here so quickly and so easily; when Mac gave me the directions, I thought I might get lost because I have no sense of direction but incredibly, here I am.

I stare up at the sign over the door and remind myself not to hesitate. I don't want to appear suspicious by hanging around outside the bank trying to summon up the courage to go inside. I put my shoulders back, take a deep breath and push open the heavy glass door and walk into the bank.

This is it.

CHAPTER ELEVEN

I feel exhilarated.

I sit and stare out of the train window as the countryside flashes by and try to contain my excitement.

I did it!

And it was so easy; once I'd walked through the doors of the bank I felt as if I *was* Katarina; I didn't feel like me at all. I didn't stumble on my words when I asked in a slightly haughty manner if I could open a new account. I didn't intend to sound so stuck up, it just came out that way. The cashier behind the desk looked at me and answered that I should have made an appointment and for a moment I felt crushed. I was so shocked that Mac hadn't thought of this because he seems so sure of the plan. But I didn't show my shock, I said *Oh really?* in a disbelieving tone and the cashier looked at me for a moment and then jumped up from her seat and said she'd see what she could do. She scurried off through a door at the back of the cashiers' counters and minutes later she reappeared and said that if I didn't mind taking a seat in the waiting area then someone would be with me shortly. I smiled and thanked her and walked to what I assume was the waiting area – four chairs in a row, opposite the counter – and sat down.

Barely five minutes later a woman about my own age came out of a door and called me into the room. I sat on the chair in front of the desk while she tapped her screen and asked me questions. I found myself chatting quite naturally to her and handing Katarina's passport over as if it was real and it belonged to me.

She was very interested when I told her about being a social media influencer and I knew that the minute I left she'd be looking up Katarina on *Instagram*. She said that she hoped I didn't mind but she just had to tell me how much she loved my jumpsuit and how fabulous it looked; I smiled and thanked her as if strangers paid me compliments all of the time.

She was impressed by *me*.

I've *never* impressed anyone in my whole life and it felt so good; this must be how Katarina feels all of the time because people are always impressed by wealth and displays of it, aren't they?

And the way she spoke to me was so different to

what I'm used to. I'm either being ordered around in a low-paid menial job by someone who thinks they're important or else I'm being told what to do by a snotty cow at the Job Centre. Very rarely am I spoken to with respect, or as if what I think matters or is of any importance. This, more than anything, has made me determined to see through whatever plan Mac has decided on.

Isn't a whole new life and a whole new me worth taking a risk for?

It is, and according to Mac there is no risk – although I'll feel a lot happier when I know exactly what it is that we're going to do.

'Is this seat taken?'

I turn from my view of the countryside to see a man standing next to me, pointing at the spare seat next to mine. He's suited and booted, as we say on the estate, a little older than me and *very* good-looking.

'No,' I say, with a smile. 'It's free.' As are lots of other seats in the carriage and they don't have anyone sitting in the window seat. He smiles a mega-watt smile showing perfect teeth and slides into the seat, giving me a waft of expensive aftershave as he does so.

I think I'm about to get chatted up.

* * *

I did get chatted up and very nice it was, too, although obviously I won't be telling Mac about it.

I even got asked out on a date – which I obviously turned down by telling him I was seeing someone – but it was *so* nice to be asked by someone so attractive. James, as I discovered his name was, was travelling to a company in our town for a business meeting and asked if I lived here. I said no, that I was visiting a friend but lived in London.

I told him my name was Katarina and it didn't even feel like a lie.

As we were chatting, I realised that I was speaking differently, more slowly and more like I imagine Katarina speaks and it hit me then; I don't have to be *Jess from the sink estate*, I can be whoever I like.

When we pull into the station, I make sure that I wait until James has got off the train before I get up because I don't want to walk out of the station with him in case Mac sees us. Mac's never shown any jealousy but he's never had any reason to because let's face it, any men who might chat me up on the estate are absolutely no threat to Mac at all. I don't know why but I just have a feeling that he wouldn't like it if he saw me with James.

I'd WhatsApped Mac when I left London so he knew what time to expect me but he never replied. I can see that he read the message almost immediately and I feel annoyed that he hasn't bothered to reply. He does that a lot when he's away so I should be used to it by now but I thought he'd at least want to know if opening the bank account had gone smoothly.

I come out of the station and walk up the steps to the short stay car park which is where he'll be waiting.

But he's not there.

There are a few people hanging around waiting to be picked up and I stand near the top of the steps and wait, feeling conspicuous every time a car pulls in and picks someone else up. Do I need to go and get the bus or should I wait? It starts to spit with rain and I have no umbrella or even a coat, just Katarina's flimsy little jacket. I pull my phone out of my pocket to WhatsApp Mac when I see him swing around the entrance into the car park. I step forward and wave at him but he doesn't drive over to me but pulls the car into the nearest parking space and kills the engine.

It's definitely raining now and I pull the jacket up over my head and jog towards the car. The *Primark* heels are starting to rub my feet and my earlier elation has vanished; I just feel pissed off that he's late and now he hasn't even noticed that I'm here. I arrive at the car and pull the door handle but the door is locked and doesn't budge. I bend down and look through the window just as Mac looks up at me with his mobile clamped to his ear. He doesn't look overjoyed to see me and it's only when he's taken his phone away from his ear and it's back in his pocket that he unlocks the doors.

'It's raining,' I say, as I clamber into the front seat and slam the door shut with more force than I intended.

'It's only spitting a bit,' Mac says, staring out of the windscreen.

I wait for him to ask me how it went at the bank but he doesn't.

'Don't you want to know how it went?' I ask, trying not to sound petulant.

There's silence for a moment and then Mac grins.

'Course I do. I'm assuming it all went to plan otherwise you'd have messaged me.'

'It did go to plan,' I say, proudly, unable to stop myself from grinning. 'Unbelievably well.'

'That's my girl,' he says, putting his hand on my leg and giving it a squeeze.

'Although there was a sticky moment when she said I should have made an appointment,' I say. 'But I blagged it and she got someone to see me straight away.'

'Great,' Mac says.

I look at him out of the corner of my eye and wonder if I'm missing something, he seems distracted and disinterested. I don't understand it, he's spent every minute of the last few days going over and over what I had to do in minute detail and now he can't be bothered to show any interest.

'Is there something wrong?' I ask.

'No, course not,' he says, giving my leg another squeeze. 'Just tired, that's all.'

He puts the car into gear and reverses out of the parking space and we zoom off out of the car park and head towards home. I open my mouth to tell him more about the bank and then close it again and we spend the rest of the journey in silence.

* * *

Mac's phone starts to ring as we pull up at the car park outside the flats.

'Go on in,' he says, pulling his mobile out of his pocket. 'I've got to take this.'

I climb out of the car and slam the door and trudge towards the flats. I'm wondering what I've done wrong because Mac is definitely off and he's never been like that before.

I wonder if he's going off me.

By the time I let myself into the flat I feel thoroughly dejected and when I walk into the lounge and see the mess in there it doesn't help. An empty glass and two coffee cups are lying on the coffee table amidst empty crisp packets and biscuit crumbs. I know that Mac is untidy so I'm used to it but the sight of the mess infuriates me and I walk straight back out of the lounge and into the bedroom. It's no better in there; the bed is unmade with the quilt trailing on the floor and I see another empty mug and a plate that has toast crumbs on it poking out from underneath it. The curtains are still closed across the window where he hasn't bothered to open them and there are various piles of clothes heaped around the floor. Normally I would pick everything up, make the bed and open the curtains but today I don't, I'm in too much of a bad mood.

By the time Mac comes in I've changed into jeans and a sweatshirt and am sitting on the sofa in the lounge. I've made no attempt to tidy any of the mess up but I don't know why not because it's not as if he'll even notice. I'll have to do it eventually because Mac definitely won't.

'I've ordered a Chinese,' he says, flopping onto the sofa next to me. 'But before it arrives tell me everything about today.'

I look at him in surprise and it must show on my face because he laughs sheepishly.

'Yeah, sorry about earlier. Had a bit of trouble with someone but it's all sorted now.'

'Oh.' Is all I manage to say.

He wraps his arm around me and pulls me close and kisses the top of my head.

'I've just a miserable sod who needs a good slap,' he murmurs. 'Just kick me next time I have a gob on.'

I relax into him and tell myself to stop sulking; everyone is allowed an off day, aren't they?

'So what was the trouble?' I ask.

'Nothing for you to worry about, just someone I'm dealing with who's a bit awkward. Come on, tell me how it went at the bank.' He sits back and looks at me expectantly.

I smile and begin from when I arrived outside the bank and he listens carefully, interrupting now and then to ask a question. By the time I've finished he's grinning and I see a different Mac from the one who picked me up from the station.

'Brilliant,' he says, as the door knocker heralds the arrival of our Chinese takeaway. 'You're amazing.' He jumps up and returns with two brown paper carrier bags and dumps them on the coffee table and begins to take out the cartons. 'You've done so well, I think you're a natural.'

I laugh but secretly think that maybe he's right, maybe I am.

I go out into the kitchen and return with plates and cutlery and we tuck into the food. I'm starving as I haven't eaten since breakfast time and even though Chinese food isn't my favourite, I eat far more than I should. I was hoping that we'd go out somewhere nice tonight and celebrate instead of eating in and I try not to feel disappointed.

I *was* all dressed up with nowhere to go; not that Mac has even noticed that I've changed my clothes. I can't help feeling a bit cheated; today was a big thing for me and tonight isn't turning out a bit like I expected.

'So,' Mac says, scooping the last forkful of rice into his mouth and dumping the plate on the coffee table. 'Time to tell you the plan.'

'But first,' he says, standing up and walking over to his holdall and unzipping it. 'We have to set up your online banking.' He pulls out a silver laptop. He comes and sits back down, opens up the laptop and fires it up. 'You've got the account details?'

'Yep.' I go into the bedroom and take the paperwork out of my bag and take it back into the lounge and give it to Mac and sit down next to him. He navigates to the bank website and clicks on the link to set up online banking.

'You'll get a text to say that I'm doing this for security,' Mac says, as he types. 'You gave them your mobile number, didn't you?'

'I did,' I say, picking up my phone. 'And that bothers me a bit, because that connects me directly to that bank account.'

'You worry too much,' Mac says. 'We can easily bin that phone and get you another one.'

I don't say anything but watch as he sets up online banking for Katarina's new account. I suggested that we get a burner phone but Mac said it wasn't necessary; he says we'll be long gone by the time anyone starts looking into mobile phone records.

'You need to accept that and confirm,' Mac says, as my mobile bleeps. I click to accept.

'Okay, that's all done, see?' He points to the screen and there it is, Katarina's new account with a three-hundred-pounds balance.

I nod and smile.

'So,' he says, logging out of the account. 'The plan.'

I sit back and wait.

'The plan is to transfer all of her savings out of her existing savings account into our new one.' He says, as if this explains everything.

'How?'

'Easy,' he says with a grin. 'Once she's safely on

holiday you go into her bank pretending to be her and hand over her the cloned card and say you want to transfer it all into a new account that you've got set up and that you'd like them to raise you a cheque. They won't send a text message or anything like that because you'll be there in person so there's no way she'll find out until she gets back. And even if they did send her a message by the time she can do anything about it we'll be long gone.'

I feel sick; I thought pretending to be Katarina was a one off but I'm going to have to do it again, only this time the stakes are much higher. What if I mess it up?

'What if I get caught?' I ask, my mouth dry.

'You won't.' Mac laughs. 'It's risk-free, there's no reason for anyone at that bank to even remotely suspect you. Why would they? You can take the passport with you in case they ask for it but trust me, no one is going to suspect you're not Katarina. This'll be the easiest hundred-and-fifty-grand ever we've never earned.'

I don't know what plan I expected but impersonating Katarina again never crossed my mind.

'How do you know she has that much?' I ask.

'Leaves her bank statements and investment stuff lying around the house for anyone to see, doesn't she?' Mac smirks. 'Stupid cow.'

'I don't know if I've got the nerve,' I admit.

'Of course you have, you did brilliantly today so

just do that again and we're made.'

I feel sick.

'Listen.' Mac slips his arm around me and pulls me close. 'Just keep in your mind what we're doing it for and you'll be fine. Focus on that and think about our new life in Spain and it'll be a breeze.'

He's right; this is for our new life away from this shitty estate.

And then it hits me.

I'm the one taking all the risk.

CHAPTER TWELVE

I didn't sleep well last night but Mac didn't have a problem, he slept like a log, snoring his head off beside me. It's strange, but I've never noticed him snoring before.

When we got up this morning, he said he had to go out but would be back tonight. He quickly drank the cup of coffee that I made him but didn't hang around to have any breakfast. He said he didn't have time but I don't know what the hurry was because he never told me.

He never tells me where he's going or what he's doing and it's not bothered me before but if we're going to have a life together, shouldn't I know a bit more about him and his life? He knows pretty much everything about my life – not that there's a lot to know – but I know barely anything about him.

We haven't talked about past relationships even though he must have had loads of girlfriends because he's drop dead gorgeous but he's never spoken about any of them, not one, and he's never asked me about mine. He says he's not interested in who's been in my life before because he says, what's the point? It's history and has nothing to do with us now.

I agreed with him because I haven't had very many relationships and they'll all been short-lived and not worth mentioning because they didn't mean anything to me. The men in my life before I met Mac were just a big disappointment and quite honestly, I'd have been embarrassed talking about them.

I hope Mac's not going to disappoint me.

I finish my toast and go into the lounge and collect the plates and rubbish from last night's takeaway and carry it all out into the kitchen. I usually tidy up before I go to bed but last night I just couldn't be bothered. The flat feels grubby and uncared for which isn't helping my mood because I can't bear living in a mess. It's not a great flat but I normally keep it clean and tidy and I like to think that it feels cosy and homely but it doesn't feel that way now.

I feel fed up and unsettled but I'm not sure why.

In an effort to improve my mood I set about cleaning the flat; I wash up the assorted cups, plates and glasses that Mac has left scattered around and then dry them and put them away. I then set about giving the kitchen a good clean and by the time I've finished it looks, and feels, much fresher. I drag the hoover out of the cupboard in the hall and give the threadbare carpets a good vacuuming. The bathroom gets cleaned too and by the time I've finished it's lunchtime and I look around at the flat and feel satisfied that it no longer looks like a pigsty. I've also put a wash on of Mac's clothes as he seems to wear something for five minutes and then throw it on the floor.

I make myself a cup of tea and settle down at the kitchen table to check Katarina's *Instagram*. She's shopping yet again; floaty, colourful kaftans for the beach, hashtag *beach cover ups*. I bought a beach cover up from *Primark* last year – not that I've been anywhere near a beach to wear it but a girl can dream, can't she? It was turquoise blue and made out of a chiffony-type material that was obviously nylon but I thought it was nice.

It was eight-pounds-ninety-nine.

I've never worn it but I will when we get to Spain.

The first kaftan that Katarina has tagged is by a designer called *Camilla Franks*, who I've never even heard of. Katarina is enthusing over how wonderful it is and what a bargain it is at only six-hundred-and-thirty-pounds.

For a kaftan.

If I felt any guilt at all about stealing from Katarina, this would kill it stone dead.

But I actually don't feel guilty at all.

I just feel scared in case I get caught.

Is that bad that I don't feel guilty at the thought of stealing someone's savings? It is bad because stealing is a crime as well as morally wrong but I can't make myself feel guilty no matter how much I try. I've no doubt that her rich husband will replace whatever we steal and she'll be no worse off and a hundred-and-fifty-thousand-pounds is peanuts to people like them. People like her never suffer or go without because there's always someone there to bail them out or give them even more stuff even though they have everything already. I see in the celebrity magazines that when these celebs go to awards ceremonies or anything like that they get given *goodie bags* with expensive gifts and beauty treatments inside that they probably don't even want.

I tap out of *Instagram* and click on the icon for the app store and download the app for the bank where I opened the account yesterday. While it downloads, I ask myself why I'm doing this and I don't have an answer. When the app opens, I hit the *sign in* button and tap in the username for the account that I opened. Mac didn't tell me the username or the password because he obviously thinks there's no reason for me to know, but I have it anyway. I watched him as he typed it in and made a note on my phone because I didn't want to forget it. When he thought I was waiting for the confirmation text from the bank I was actually typing in the username and password in *notes*.

I've very good at reading stuff upside-down and also watching what keys are hit when someone's typing. Or both, sometimes. I watched Beatrice at the Job Centre type in her password whilst I was sitting opposite her and I know what that is too; *Samson22?&z*. I'm guessing that's her cat. Not that her password is of any use to me at all but it's all good practice and harmless fun.

The account opens and there's nothing new to see and why would there be? I don't have any reason to look but I just like to be kept in the loop, and it is my name on the account, when all said and done. The account is showing the three-hundred-pounds that I paid in yesterday.

When I was telling Mac how the trip to the bank went, I didn't tell him that the bank doesn't normally accept cash to open an account. Due to money laundering regulations they prefer to take the deposit from an existing debit card. When she told me this, I thought for a moment that I'd have to make an excuse and leave but I put on a bewildered expression when she said it. I then looked at her blankly as if I didn't understand and repeated that *I'd really like to get rid of the surplus cash I'd drawn out*. She bit her lip and then disappeared out of the office and came back several minutes later and said that cash would be fine.

That makes two things that Mac got wrong; we should have made an appointment and the bank doesn't normally accept cash. I'm surprised about this because I thought Mac knew exactly what he was doing but two mistakes isn't good even though I managed to overcome them.

He's not quite as perfect as I thought he was; he doesn't know *everything*.

And then there's the mobile phone thing; the bank have *my* mobile phone number and not Mac's so when Katarina calls the police and reports the theft, that telephone number is going to lead straight back to me. I'll be a wanted person because the police will know everything about me and although we'll be in Spain, they'll be able to track me down or as soon as I come back to the UK I'll be arrested. I just don't understand why we didn't buy a burner phone and use it; there's no way that phone could have been traced to me if we'd done that. I can't understand why Mac didn't think of this.

I should have insisted and not assumed that he knew everything.

I'm beginning to think that I've been a bit stupid.

But it's not too late; aside from opening an account in someone else's name I haven't stolen any money.

Yet.

I toss my mobile onto the table and stare into space. If I don't go through with this, I'll lose Mac for sure and there'll be no new life in Spain and I'll be stuck here forever.

I have to choose; take the risk and hope that I can hide away in Spain or live here in this grubby flat for ever, alone and working minimum wage jobs because I'm never likely to meet anyone like Mac again. Mac might not be perfect but who is? I'm certainly not; there are things about me that aren't good in any way, shape or form so why do I expect him to be perfect and never make a mistake?

I push the chair back and stand up and wander aimlessly around the flat, as if movement will somehow provide the answer. I stand in the lounge and stare out of the window at the car park below; the March wind is blowing the rubbish around and plastic carrier bags and discarded rubbish tumble through the air. A rusting Land Rover without wheels is balanced on bricks in the space right in front of the entrance. It's been there for as long as I can remember. Three men are loitering in front of the bin store; one of them is wearing a black *Harrington* jacket and grubby jeans and I recognise the bald head of Seamus. No doubt he's *helping out his mates* with some weed or other type of drug.

Nobody in their right mind would choose to live here if they didn't have to.

Do I really want to spend the rest of my life here? Because that's the choice; take a big risk or settle for this.

I have to take the risk.

I turn around and look around the lounge, I want more than a shabby sofa from a second-hand shop and Mum's old coffee table, more than a threadbare carpet that's most likely been in this flat since it was built.

I want to buy new, decent things and have a new life.

I have to take the risk. And in the big scheme of things, a hundred-and-fifty-thousand-pounds is small fry; the police will hardly be classing me as an international criminal mastermind and pulling out all of the stops to track me down.

I *can* do it, I *have* to do it.

And as I congratulate myself on making the right decision, I look at the coffee table and suddenly remember what it is that's been niggling at the back of my mind. On the day that I came back for my purse, Mac was talking on his mobile in the bedroom. I remember the feeling as I left that there was something important that I was missing.

I now know what it was.

As I picked up my purse from the clutter on the coffee table, Mac's mobile phone was lying next to it. If his mobile was on the table, how could he be using it in the bedroom?

He couldn't.

Which means that Mac has another mobile phone.

One that he's kept a secret from me.

CHAPTER THIRTEEN

When Mac came home last night, I didn't ask him if he had two phones because I wanted to think things over. I wanted to be sure that I'm not over-reacting.

There could be a perfectly reasonable explanation for him having two mobile phones because some people do.

Like drug dealers.

He's not a drug dealer but Mum's right, he is a crook, so it's quite feasible for him to have two mobiles and I should just come out and ask him, but I won't.

I'd rather find out for myself.

This is one of my faults; I don't ever ask outright when it's something like this because, as I've said before, I have trust issues. I need to find out for myself otherwise I won't be happy that I'm being told the truth. It's one of the reasons why my previous relationships have never lasted very long. Dani exaggerated by saying that I *go full psycho* when what she really means is that when someone treats me badly, then I don't take it well. I'm not like Dani, who lets Jake cheat on her constantly and then takes him back and forgives him until he does it again.

I'm just not made like that.

Cheat on me or treat me badly and you're gone, end of. I love Mac and I want to be able to trust him but I have to prove things for myself because that's the way I'm made.

But I'm getting ahead of myself; the first thing I have to do is find the phone.

'What time is it?' Mac mumbles from underneath the quilt next to me.

I reach my hand out and grab my phone from the bedside table.

'Quarter to eight,' I say.

'Shit. I'd better get up.' Mac pulls himself up onto his elbows and blinks. 'I'm meeting my contact at ten.'

'You've got plenty of time,' I say.

'No, I haven't, it's in London,' he says, sitting upright and throwing the duvet back. He swings his legs out of bed and rests his elbows on his knees and rubs his face.

'Not feeling great?' I ask.

'Just tired,' he says.

He didn't get back until gone eleven last night;

I'd almost given up hope of him coming home and was getting ready for bed. He said that his contact had been hard to track down and that he'd almost given up on meeting him but then had managed to track him down to a pub. When I asked him what he had to see him about, he said that he had to make sure he could get into Katarina's house when she was on holiday. He needed someone who knew about burglar alarms because he wouldn't be able to just sneak in through the back garden and an unlocked door like he had before.

'So why have you got to meet him again today?' I ask, sitting up in bed.

Mac looks round at me and narrows his eyes and for a weird moment I think that he's going to tell me to mind my own business.

'The code,' he says, flatly.

'For what?' I look at him blankly.

'For the alarm, obviously.'

'Oh, yeah,' I giggle.

He stands up and stretches his arms over his head with a grunt and then saunters across the bedroom and into the hallway and I hear him pad along to the bathroom. Again, I wonder if he's going off me because he's been in a weird mood the last few days; maybe the novelty of me has worn off after two months. It hasn't helped that we haven't had sex because I've turned him down; I have my period and chronic stomach ache and I don't actually feel like it. I've never actually refused him before because my last periods coincided with him working away.

Maybe he doesn't love me; maybe it's just sex for him.

But he didn't actually say he loved me, did he? Maybe I just wanted to think that he did. I'm being oversensitive; I can't expect the honeymoon period to last forever, can I? This is real-life, bad moods and all.

I throw back the quilt and run quietly to the door and look out into the hallway. The bathroom door is closed and the shower isn't running yet so he must be having a shave. He'll be ages yet so I have plenty of time. My heart starts to pound and I take a few deep breaths; I need to be calm and methodical because there aren't many places in the bedroom where he could hide a phone. Finding it shouldn't take too long.

It must be in the bedroom because he was using it in here; if I can't find it, I'll check his bag but I need to do it while he's here because he'll take the other phone with him.

I squat on the floor and look underneath the bed; apart from a few balls of fluff there's nothing. I look around the room; the chest of drawers is full of my stuff except for the bottom drawer which I've given to him for his clothes. I cross the room and quietly pull the drawer open and put my hand in and run it through the drawer. There's nothing in there except for underpants, socks and a few t-shirts.

The bedside tables are simple tables with a

shelf underneath and they have nothing on them except for two rickety lamps. That only leaves the wardrobe unless he's pulled up a floorboard and hidden it underneath the floor. I ponder this for a moment and then decide that the carpet is fitted so it wouldn't be possible. I quietly open the wardrobe doors and run my hands down the clothes hanging inside, paying particular attention to any pockets. Nothing. I kneel down and check all of the shoes in the bottom, feeling inside each one even though most of them are mine. I pull each pair upwards to check underneath them to make sure I haven't missed anything but there's nothing.

That's it; there's nowhere else in this room to hide a phone.

I scan the room looking for inspiration but I can't see any other possible hiding place. The bottom of the chest of drawers touches the carpet and there's no room to put anything underneath and the wardrobe is the same.

Unless.

I walk over to the wardrobe and stand at the side and stand on tiptoes. I reach up and feel along the top with my fingers. As I touch the part nearest the wall, I feel the unmistakable shape of a mobile phone. I take hold of it and slowly bring it down, listening for any movement from the bathroom as I do so.

For a moment I think that it's the phone that he always uses because it's identical; a black iPhone 13. I swipe the screen and as I expected, it's locked.

I tap in the code that I've seen Mac use so often on his other phone, 3112. The screen immediately unlocks and I can't help smiling to myself, people are so predictable. I go straight to contacts, not really sure what I'm going to find. As it turns out, not very much.

There are no names in the contacts, just the letter X.

And one number.

I stare at the number and then quickly cross to the bed, grab my own phone from the bedside table and take a picture of the screen. I hear the sound of the bathroom door opening and I quickly run to the wardrobe and slip the mobile phone back onto the top where I found it. I can hear Mac's feet padding down the hallway and I run to the bed and have just laid down as he walks back into the room.

'Feel better?' I ask.

He grunts a reply and walks over to the chest of drawers and opens the bottom drawer and pulls out a pair of underpants. He drops the towel on the floor where he stands and puts the pants on and crosses to the wardrobe, leaving the drawer hanging open.

How did I ever think he was perfect and why would he be? No one is perfect, it's a fact, and our relationship is entering a new phase of reality because no one can stay in the infatuation stage forever, it's not possible.

Mac rifles through the hangers looking for something to wear, knocking one of my dresses off the hanger in the process. He pulls a pair of jeans off a hanger and puts them on, then repeats the process a second time, grabbing a sweatshirt which he pulls over his head. Once dressed he turns and looks at me.

'You not getting up?' he asks.

'In a while,' I say. I know that he wants me out of the room so he can retrieve his phone. Maybe I should have moved it and given him a fright; maybe then he'd tell me the truth about what it's for if I asked him.

'Could you make me a coffee?' he asks, with a smile. 'I still need waking up.'

'Okay,' I say, getting out of bed and putting my dressing gown on. 'Do you want toast as well?'

He picks his watch up from the top of the chest of drawers and looks at it.

'That would be good,' he says. 'I've just got time.'

I take my time walking out of the room knowing that he's itching to retrieve his phone. When I get to the kitchen, I think about going back into the bedroom just to startle him but I stop myself; I can pretend to myself that I'm fine with it all but I'm not; I'm so not.

I put the kettle on and spoon coffee into mugs and put bread in the toaster and stand and stare out of the window. The next thing I know, Mac is standing behind me and has looped his arms around my waist and is nuzzling my neck.

'Penny for them?' he asks.

'I'm just imagining not having to live

somewhere where it constantly rains,' I lie.

'It won't be long,' he says. 'And you and I will be out of here.'

I turn around to face him and put my arms around his neck and stare up at him.

'Really?' I say. 'You really think we can do this?'

'We're doing it already, we're half way there.'

I sigh and rest my head against him and close my eyes. I wish I hadn't remembered about the phone and I wish I hadn't found the bloody thing. I was happy before I started doubting him and now, I feel on edge and unsettled. Why do I find it so difficult to trust anyone?

'You're not having second thoughts, are you?' Mac asks, quietly.

'No, of course not.'

'That's my girl.'

We stand in silence for several moments and I revel in the warmth of his body.

'Come on, then, gorgeous,' Mac says, slowly releasing his hold on me. 'Make your man a coffee.'

I like it when he says he's my man.

I make the coffees and put them on the table and press the lever down on the toaster. Once it pops, I slather butter and marmalade on it and put the plate down in front of Mac.

'You not having any?' he asks, taking an enormous bite.

'I'll have something later,' I say, taking a sip of my coffee.

'I'll share,' he says, offering me the plate.

'Because anything that's mine is yours.'

I take half a slice and bite into it.

He does love me.

Just because he was in a funny mood yesterday doesn't mean that he doesn't love me and so what if he has two phones? He's a ducker and diver and two mobile phones is almost obligatory in that world. Christ, even Seamus has two mobiles despite the fact that he barely knows how to even use one. When Mac comes back tonight, I'm just going to come right out and ask him about the mobile phone and put my mind at rest.

My trust issues have got the better of me again but I'm determined that this time I'm not going to ruin something good by being suspicious all the time. Mac knows what he's doing and he wouldn't have asked me to get a passport if he didn't want me to go to Spain with him, would he?

No, of course he wouldn't.

Get a grip, Jess, and stop going full psycho like you always do.

'I thought we could go up town tonight,' Mac says, shoving the last piece of toast into his mouth. 'Celebrate your success at the bank. We could try that new Italian place that you've been itching to go to. Then maybe go onto a club afterwards. Make a night of it.'

'I'd love that.'

'Great, I'll be back by six at the latest so I'll book a table for seven-thirty.'

'Perfect,' I say.

'Got to go, now.' He pushes the chair back and stands up. 'I'll see you later.' He walks out into the hallway, kissing me quickly on the lips as he goes.

I hear the front door close and I sit back in the chair and sip my coffee. I'm such a suspicious idiot; I constantly try to sabotage my own happiness but I'm not doing it anymore. I want to trust Mac; I don't want my trust issues to ruin what we have.

I pick up my phone and open up Katarina's *Instagram*. Surprisingly, she's not posted anything yet, although it is only half-past-eight so maybe that's a bit early even for her. I scroll through her old posts, zooming in on different ones as I go. She posts every single bit of her life and I wonder if she does anything without her phone camera in her hand.

Going to the toilet and having a bath is probably the only thing she doesn't post; she even takes pictures of herself putting make-up on although I'm sure she uses a filter to make herself look perfect because no one can look that good without make-up.

Not even my double.

It's strange, because although she looks exactly like me, the more I look at her the less I feel like her. It must be because she has such a different life from me; she looks like me but that's all. She's vain, spoilt, entitled and everything that I'm not.

I don't like her.

I continue aimlessly scrolling, beyond bored but unable to stop. I'll stop in a minute, I keep telling myself, I'll go and get showered and brush my teeth and get dressed. But still I keep scrolling as if her *Instagram* account has the answers to everything I ever wanted to know.

And then I stop in shock.

I zoom in.

I can't breathe.

Because there it is, right in front of me, and I wonder how I never noticed before.

It can't be.

But it is.

CHAPTER FOURTEEN

We had a fabulous meal at the Dolce Vita last night and it was well worth the wait to go there, my Spaghetti Carbonara was delicious and the Tiramisu was the best I've ever had. Not that I've had many, because truthfully, it only had to be better than a McDonalds to get my vote.

Mac was true to his word and was home by six-o-clock so had plenty of time to get showered and changed before we went out. He suggested we get a cab into town so we could both have a few drinks to celebrate my bank account success. Although I had no intention of getting drunk, I agreed, because it wasn't as if I could drive us there and there's no way that Mac would get on a bus.

The restaurant gave us the best table at the front in the window alcove. I know for a fact that they only ever put people at that table if they look really good because the restaurant want passers-by to be impressed and to entice people in. I felt as if we were famous celebs when we were shown to our seats. Mac and I did look pretty good; Mac dressed casually in a shirt, trousers and jacket but he just makes everything he wears look so good. He has a way of wearing the clothes so that they don't wear him. I wore the blue jumpsuit and jacket that I wore to the bank but instead of the heels that were rubbing my feet I wore my favourite ankle boots. The waiter couldn't do enough for us and was obviously hoping for a big tip as Mac ordered an expensive bottle of champagne rather than wine.

The place was packed because it was a Saturday night and the restaurant is still new and popular. I sat there and thought; *this* must be what it's what it's like to have money and to do whatever you want. Katarina probably goes to a restaurant like this every night and thinks nothing of it.

We went onto *Vadims* afterwards which was where Mac and I first met. There was a long queue to get in when we arrived and I thought we'd be waiting ages but Mac simply walked up to the doorman and spoke quietly to him and then they let us in. Honestly, I definitely felt like a celeb then; I don't know whether he slipped the doorman some money but whatever it was it worked.

Whenever I'd been to *Vadims* before I met Mac, we'd always go early because as long as you're dressed decently, they'll likely to let you in if you're a good looking girl as they like the girl-to-guy ratio high. As the night goes on and it gets later the doormen get fussier about who gets admitted.

We'd only just arrived at the bar and were waiting to be served when who should we bump into but Dani and Taylor. I could see them looking at Mac and I with envy because they're completely rubbish at hiding their feelings. Dani was a bit embarrassing because she fawned all over Mac as if he was a god, or something. She didn't care that I was with him, probably because she was already half-cut because she'd obviously pre-loaded at home. I felt a bit annoyed with her but Mac was very charming to her which surprised me a bit. No one would have known that he actually found her drunkenness disgusting – he told me this when we got home – so I think he's made a conquest there.

Taylor had a nerdy looking guy called Simon trailing around behind her like a puppy dog. She's apparently been seeing him for over a month now even though he didn't look like her usual type at all. She normally goes for the muscle-bound, on-steroids type who wear wife-beater t-shirts even in the middle of winter to show off their muscles. Simon was a bit of a departure for her but they seemed quite sweet together, though, even if he did look a bit of a wimp. Which just shows that not everything is about looks.

Mac bought everyone a drink and went out of his way to be charming to them. I was a bit surprised because I thought that he'd make no secret of the fact that they weren't his type. He's referred to Dani and Taylor as *a bit low-rent* and his attitude is that there's no point in bothering with people that you don't like and have nothing in common with. He's been quite open about not liking Mum and has made no effort to get on with her at all and *she's* my mother. Maybe he has a thing about parents, because the way he talked about his own parents wasn't very nice.

Anyway, despite what I'd discovered on Katarina's *Instagram*, we had a very good night so I must be a very good actress. When we were in the cab on the way home he was all over me, holding my hand and kissing me. In all honesty I wanted to tell him to *fuck off* but I managed to stop myself because I don't want to do anything rash.

When we got out of the cab and it had driven off, Mac caught hold of me as I started to walk towards the flats and he put his arms around me and held me tightly. We stayed like this for several minutes and then he pulled away from me and stared at me seriously for a moment as if he was thinking about something. Then he put his fingers underneath my chin, tilted my face up towards him and kissed me softly on the lips. It was a very romantic moment even though it wasn't the most romantic of settings. The broken flag-stoned path next to the car park just outside the flats isn't exactly pretty but anyway, he looked into my eyes and told me that he loved me.

How I've longed to hear those words over

the last couple of months; how I've dreamed of the moment when Mac would finally profess his feelings for me. There are so many times I've day-dreamed about how wonderful it would be when it actually happened.

And it was romantic.

It didn't sound like a lie; if I hadn't known the truth I would have believed him.

I longed to believe him.

Of course, I didn't spoil the moment, I gazed up at him and smiled and told him that I loved him, too, and then we kissed and held each other tightly as people in love do.

And it's such a shame, it really is, because it could all have been so very different but there it is, that's the way things are and my problem with trusting anyone has been proved right, yet again.

It's like I always say; just because you're paranoid it doesn't mean they're not out to get you.

* * *

Mac's going away for a few days tomorrow to *finalise things* but I wish it was today because I can't stand looking at him. I wonder what it is he's actually going away for because I don't know what to believe anymore.

This is the trouble, once you know something, you can't un-know it and now every time I look at him, I just want to shout *liar* at him. He's actually making it worse because he's being so nice to me and I can't bear being in the same room as him. I was glad that I had the excuse of my period last night so that I didn't have to have sex with him; whereas once I couldn't get enough of him now, I don't want him to touch me.

I feel so used.

I need to go out and get away from him or else I'm going to do something I regret. I go into the lounge and Mac's lounging on the sofa watching TV and the place looks like a pigsty with all his clutter and rubbish lying around. His huge holdall is lying by the wall and I feel a sudden urge to go over and repeatedly kick it. Mac looks up at me and smiles and somehow, I manage to stretch my lips into a suitable response.

'I'm going to the shop,' I say. 'Do you want anything?'

'I wouldn't mind a couple of beers,' he says. 'You okay?'

'Fine,' I say, with a smile. 'Just got a bit of a headache. I need some fresh air.' Maybe I'm not such a good actress as I think.

He seems satisfied with my reply and turns his gaze back to the TV screen and I go out to the hallway and put my jacket on. I call out *bye* as I let myself out of the front door and when I've closed the door behind me, I stand for a moment outside and wonder what on earth I'm going to do.

I need to think and I can't do it here. I zip up my jacket and march down the corridor and down the stairs, thinking back over what I discovered yesterday.

Mac must think that I'm stupid, and up until now, I have been. Or perhaps I'm being too hard on myself. He must have *some* feelings for me because everything can't have been fake.

Unless he's a psychopath; because they don't have any feelings for anyone but themselves.

I've been too trusting, believing everything that he's ever said to me. I thought that no one could ever fool me because despite my trust issues, I've always thought myself cleverer than others.

How blind love has made me.

Even when confronted by the fact that he has two mobile phones, one of them a secret, I was still prepared to give him the benefit of the doubt. But what I found out yesterday has blown all of that out of the water because there is no doubt at all that he's lied to me.

I thought that we were going to steal from Katarina so we could start our new life together but that's not the case; I'm the one who's been set up.

When I scrolled through Katarina's posts yesterday, I stopped on a photograph she'd posted of the clutter and tools from the builders who've been refitting her bathrooms. I'd seen the post before and marvelled at the fact that she'd post anything as dreary as battered looking tools and assorted junk. There was nothing exciting in the photograph except that what I hadn't noticed before was the holdall propping up some of the tools at the side of the picture.

The holdall was Mac's.

Not one just like it but the exact one.

Yes, there are probably lots of holdalls just like it but they wouldn't all have the same initials stitched in red on each handle, would they?

JJM. John James MacDonald.

Possibly someone could have the same initials but there's also a big scuff mark down the middle panel of the holdall and the one in the photograph had the *exact* same scuff mark.

And once I'd seen that I looked at the date Katarina posted it and I felt sick.

It was before Mac and I met, months before.

When he saw me that night in *Vadims*, the reason he couldn't take his eyes off me was because he saw that I looked like Katarina and he thought that I could be useful.

The competition prize, the chance meeting on the train, it was all a set up. He knew that Katarina would be on that train and he made sure I was. And I thought that I was the smart one; feeling so pleased with myself that I'd found out Katarina's name.

It would laughable if it wasn't so tragic.

I don't know exactly what he has planned but I know that it's going to involve transferring money to the bank account that I set up. Opening that bank account and using my own mobile phone number is going to come back to haunt me and I'm going to take the fall for it.

I could tell Mac that I know what he's done but I'm afraid to, because he's proved that he's ruthless by his treatment of me and I don't quite know what he'll do.

If he can pretend to love me yet set me up, what else is he capable of?

I could go to the police but how would I explain using a fake passport to open a bank account? I can't; I'm trapped and have no idea how to get out of it.

As I walk away into the parade of shops I stop and pull out my mobile phone. I scroll through the photographs until I reach the picture I took of the telephone number in Mac's secret phone. Making sure to block my own number, I tap the number into the keypad, checking several times that I've entered the right number.

She may not answer; a lot of people won't answer a call from a withheld number but I'm hoping she will. I already know that Mac is a liar but I need this one last piece of evidence to convince me that I'm not going mad.

I press the call button.

The call connects and starts to ring and just when I think that she's not going to answer, she picks up the call.

'Hello?' a voice says.

'Hello,' I say. 'Is that Mrs Hepworth-Jones?'

'Speaking,' she replies.

And now there is no doubt.

It's Katarina.

I press the *end call* button and wonder what the hell I'm going to do.

CHAPTER FIFTEEN

Mac's gone away for a few days to finalise things. It's a relief I no longer have to look at him because each time he smiles at me I want to punch him.

I suppose this is what Dani means when she says I go *full psycho*; although I've never actually been physically violent to anyone before but for Mac, I'd make an exception.

I'm not vindictive but if someone has crossed or cheated on me, I feel compelled to get my revenge in some way. The revenge may be small and never traced to me but I always feel better to know that somehow, with a word to the right person or an anonymous phone call to someone in the know, I've made life difficult or unpleasant for whoever crossed me for a short while. Most people who live around here are involved in something dodgy in one way or another so it's not difficult to find some way to get them into trouble.

I don't know what that says about me, wanting revenge. Nothing good, I should think.

And I never tell anyone what I've done – those trust issues again – but Dani is always first with the latest gossip and always knows what's going on before anyone else – even Mum – and she can't wait to tell me when one of my ex's is in the shit. She'll imply that I had something to do with whatever misfortune has befallen them and just laughs when I protest that it had nothing to do with me.

Maybe she's a lot brighter than I give her credit for.

But I don't think that sort of revenge will be possible with Mac; he's not the average layabout from this estate, he's different. It's going to take all of my effort and presence of mind to make sure that I don't end up paying the price for something that he's done. I thought that I loved him with all my heart but now I hate him for what he's done to me and when I think of him it's with hatred.

Who knew that love could turn to hate so quickly?

I knew. It's happened to me before and my feelings are like a switch; betray me and I'll hate you with as much passion as I loved you.

I've wasted my love on him and am struggling to understand how he could lie so convincingly to my face when he's plotting my downfall behind my back. I remember how we'd lie in bed together, how close we felt and how we seemed to know what the other was thinking.

All a lie.

I've gone over and over it in my mind, wondering how it's going to happen and what Mac is actually going to do. I feel sick and I wish there was someone I could turn to but there isn't; I'm in this on my own and I have no one to help me.

The only thing that I know for sure is that whatever is going to happen will be soon. Katarina goes on holiday tomorrow and the bank card will arrive in the next few days and I'll be required to go to the bank again and transfer the funds. This will seal my fate.

I'm going to refuse to do it but what will happen to me then?

What will Mac do to me?

I've racked my brains to try and work out what Mac's plan it. Is Mac blackmailing Katarina? Is he making sure that there's no possibility of the money she's paying him being traced to him? I know that once I've transferred the money, he'll transfer it straight into another account using online banking. He'll be long gone before the police have a chance to catch him. I wonder why he wanted me to get a passport if it was all a lie. But then I remember that it has to look to the police as if I intended taking the money and running.

But why would he need to look as if I'd stolen it? Because if he's blackmailing her, she's hardly going to report it to the police.

Or maybe Mac and Katarina are in it together – but I don't see how that can be; why do I need to be involved if she's going to leave her husband and run off with Mac?

None of it makes sense.

I could contact Katarina.

But what if she *is* in on it? Because she was on the train the day, I went to London so is involved or did Mac know that she'd be there? She posts everything she does or is planning to do on *Instagram* so he could easily have seen it on there, despite his lies about never looking at social media.

I daren't contact her in case she's involved with Mac. I feel frozen with indecision.

I'm well and truly stuck and the only thing left for me to do is to try and think of a way to get myself out of this situation.

If I only knew what the situation actually is.

I need a miracle

* * *

Mum is blowing up my phone again so I suppose I'll have to go and see her or else she'll be round here for hours and hours. And it's not as if I have anything else to do except brood and worry. I don't know why she's become so needy lately; every time we see each other we end up arguing so I don't know why we bother.

At least it'll get me out of the flat for a while

because I've been pacing around all morning and have achieved precisely nothing. I check my phone again to see if Mac has WhatsApped but there's nothing. That's not unusual and what do I want him to say? I suppose I'm just waiting for things to start.

I click onto Katarina's *Instagram* account to see what she's posted today. I've usually checked her account many times by this time but since discovering Mac's betrayal I can hardly bear to look at it. This is the first time I've looked since yesterday morning. I stare at the screen and refresh it as I can't quite understand what I'm seeing.

Or rather, not seeing.

She hasn't posted at all today and it's gone one o'clock in the afternoon. I scroll back through her account and look at her posts; her last post was yesterday afternoon at five o'clock and since then, nothing.

Maybe she's busy because she's going on holiday tomorrow and she doesn't have time to post.

No, I can't see that at all; she *lives* for *Instagram*. I was expecting her to be posting every single item that she puts in her suitcase with a hashtag for every designer item of clothing that she's taking with her.

It doesn't make any sense at all and without her constant posts I have no idea what she's doing or where she is.

I get up from the kitchen chair and stare out of the window as if somehow the drizzle outside will supply the answer.

It doesn't.

Why stop posting now?

Maybe she's not able to post anything, maybe it's not a choice.

Maybe she's dead.

Maybe Mac has killed her.

These thoughts pop into my head out of nowhere and I wonder if I'm truly going mad. Do I really think that Mac is capable of murder?

I don't know; I just remember the way he looks sometimes.

I think he's capable of anything.

But why would he murder her – it makes no sense.

My head is aching with the effort of trying to control my thoughts; everything is going round and round in my head on a loop and making no sense at all and getting precisely nowhere. I wish that I could wake up from this nightmare and go back to my boring, humdrum life.

I wish that I'd never met Mac.

I stare down at the car park and watch the familiar figure of Seamus loitering by the bins as he peddles his wares. My life may have exploded but there are still some certainties in my life; Seamus will always be *sorting out* his friends and Mum will always have a stolen bagful of *Primark's* latest arrivals hidden underneath her bed, waiting to be sold for peanuts down the pub.

Some things never change and right now I'd give anything to go back to the life I had before I met Mac because what I had seems perfect. I used to think that I had the worst life but now I realise that I had the freedom to do anything that I wanted. I wasted it by being lazy and waiting for something to happen to take me away from this life.

Seamus's 'friends' wander off and he lingers by the bins, hands in pockets, hood pulled over his head, hopeful of more sales to come. I stand and watch him for a moment and then slip my phone into my jeans pocket and go out to the hall and put my trainers on. I grab my jacket from the hook and let myself out of the door and hurry along the corridor to the stairs, a small sprig of hope starting to grow inside me.

As I hurry down the stairs as quickly as I can, I concentrate on the germ of an idea growing in my mind.

Perhaps all is not lost.

CHAPTER SIXTEEN

I woke up this morning to a WhatsApp message from Mac:

Will ring you later

This is the first message that I've received from him; he left to *finalise things* on Monday and it's now Wednesday, two whole days without any contact from him at all which has felt more like three weeks. Before he left, he said that he wouldn't message anything about what we're doing in case the messages *fall into the wrong hands*. I assume he means the police, because he won't want anything that's going to incriminate *him* on my phone. I wonder if his own mobile phone is even registered to him; maybe he's going to discard that mobile along with me. Maybe he has more than two mobile phones.

I could ring him, of course, but besides already

knowing that he won't answer, I also don't want to make him suspicious. I've never rung him before when he's been away so I need to continue being the same, pliable, do-as-I'm-told Jess that he's come to *not* love and *not* treasure. I don't want to give him any idea that I know he's tricked me.

I'm guessing that when he rings me it'll be to tell me that I have to go to the bank and transfer the cash from Katarina's account into the fake one I opened. For that I'm going to need the bank card which should have been sent to Katarina's house by now. I assume Mac has broken into her house and has this in his possession but I'll also need the cloned card of the account it's being transferred from to be able to do it.

Or is that all a lie too? Does he have something completely different planned for me to do that has nothing to do with transferring money?

I wish I knew.

But what I do know is that I can't sit around here all day waiting for him to call, I need to *do* something. I've spent the last three days wandering around this flat from room to room in a state of anxiety, my stomach churning and my head spinning.

I can't do it anymore.

I need this to be over.

I flick onto Katarina's *Instagram* for what seems like the hundredth time today to see that she still hasn't posted anything since Sunday.

Right, that's it, no more.

I go into the hallway and take my mini rucksack down from the peg and check that my purse is inside. I slip my mobile phone into the bag and then go into the bedroom. I have no idea what is going to happen so I have to be prepared for anything. I'm going to take my passport with me even though I don't see any realistic chance of me being able to use it; somehow, the thought of me fleeing the country and going abroad seems like a far-fetched joke. The furthest place that I've been on my own is London.

To think that when I applied for that passport I had such dreams of Mac and I living in Spain. How stupid and gullible was I?

I cross the room to the chest of drawers and pull the top drawer open and put my hand in and feel around underneath my underwear. After several minutes I can't seem to put my hand on it so I pull the drawer out as far as it will go and remove all of my underwear and the two pregnancy tests and put them on the top.

The drawer is completely empty.

My passport isn't in there.

I proceed to put everything back in the drawer, carefully going through every item to make sure the passport hasn't caught on something.

It hasn't.

Which can only mean one thing; Mac has taken my passport.

Why would he need it?

Fear clutches at my insides and I try desperately

to think what Mac has planned but draw a blank; I have no clue.

As I stand there staring at my underwear drawer, I hear the sound of my mobile phone ringing from inside the rucksack. I rummage in the bag and grab my phone and then drop it on the floor in my panic. I pick it up and look at the screen, half expecting to see *Mum* flashing from the screen at me but it's Mac. I tap to accept the call.

'Hello,' I say, my mouth suddenly dry.

'Hey,' Mac says, sounding as if we spoke only minutes ago, not days. 'We're all set, babe.'

'Are we?' I ask, my voice coming out in a whisper.

Mac laughs and a feeling of pure hatred bubbles up inside me.

'So,' he says. 'Get on a train and come to Katarina's house this afternoon and we'll go to the bank tomorrow.'

'Why?' I ask. 'Why do I need to come to Katarina's? Why don't we just go straight to the bank?'

'I thought we could spend the night here,' he says, huskily. 'We can get down and dirty in their super-sized bed, show it some real action. Get used to living in luxury.'

'I can't find my passport,' I blurt out, ignoring what he's said.

'I've got it,' he says, without missing a beat.

'Why?' I demand.

'For the flights to Spain tomorrow night.'

'What do you mean,' I ask. 'How can you need it before we even get on the plane?'

He laughs again and I put my hand over my mouth to stop myself from shouting *liar* at him.

'I forget you've never been abroad. When you book a flight you need passport numbers and dates of birth for the tickets. Why else would I take it?' he asks, quietly.

I don't answer, not trusting myself to speak.

'Hey, what's wrong?' he asks. 'There's no need to get stressed, everything will be fine.'

He sounds so normal, so *loving*. For a brief moment I wonder if I'm imagining his betrayal but then reality brings me back down to earth.

'What's up, Jess?' he asks, concern in his voice.

'Nothing,' I mumble, stifling a sudden urge to cry.

'Look, I'm sorry I haven't been able to contact you but it's been a bit of a few days but everything's sorted now.'

'Okay,' I manage to say.

'You sure? We're nearly there, babe, we're so close. Don't back out on me now.'

'I won't,' I say. 'I'm just nervous, that's all.'

'Don't be, it'll go like clockwork. In a couple of days we'll be sunning ourselves on a beach in Spain and this shithole of a country will be a distant memory.'

'Can't wait,' I say.

'Nor me,' he says, huskily. 'We've got some celebrating to do.'

Somehow, I manage to giggle like the old Jess would have done and if I didn't hate him so much I'd be impressed at what a good liar he is. Although I'm a pretty good liar myself.

'And don't bother packing anything. We're buying everything new when we get there; I don't want any reminders of this miserable country.'

'Nor me,' I say.

'Right, gotta go,' he says. 'See you later. Remember, wait until it's dark and then come to the front door and ring the bell and I'll let you in.'

'Okay.'

'Love you,' he says, as he hangs up the phone.

'Love you more,' I answer.

* * *

I've tied my hair up in a ponytail and I have a mask over the bottom half of my face. I've dressed in jeans, trainers and a black sweatshirt with a navy, three-quarter-length nylon cagoule over the top. I found the cagoule in the bottom of the wardrobe with a pile of other stolen *Primark* clothes that Mum has given me over the years. Unable to bring myself to throw out brand new clothes as it seemed so wasteful, I also couldn't bring myself to wear any of them as they're so completely hideous. Little did I know that one day they would come in useful.

Any resemblance between me and Katarina would be very hard to spot right now. I'm sure that

Katarina would rather be dead than wear a nylon cagoule.

Maybe she is dead.

Although I don't think she is. I've scoured all the online newspapers and there's no mention of her being murdered so I think that my imagination has been running away with me. She's rich, she's married, she has friends, she's middle-class and she would be missed so there's no way she could just disappear off the face of the earth. The most likely explanation is that she went on holiday yesterday and is far, far away and has no decent Wi-Fi connection to post her pointless *Instagram* posts.

Not that she matters now, it's Mac that I have to deal with.

The train pulls into the station and my stomach flips over; this is it. I've a fair bit of walking to do to get to her house and I've no idea if I'll be back at the station tonight to get the train home.

I've no idea of anything much.

I clamber off the train and head out of the station and stop when I get out onto the street. I take my phone out and open up *Google* maps and check the way to Katarina's house. I've tried to memorise it so that I don't need to keep looking but now I'm here I can see that I'm going to have to check it constantly because the real streets look very different to a map.

I set off at a pace, thankful that the evenings are staying lighter for longer. I think I'd have real trouble if I had to find her street in the dark. I could get a cab but I feel the need to walk to try and clear my head. It's further than I thought and by the time I arrive at Katarina's street I've been walking for over an hour and the light is starting to fade.

The houses don't look the same as they did on street view although they obviously are the same. I walk along the pavement on the opposite side of the street to Katarina's house and I miss it the first time and have to retrace my steps. There's no sign of Mac's car on the driveway but he'd hardly advertise the fact that he was in the house by parking it there, would he? He'll have parked it in a nearby street where it won't be noticed.

I wander into the next street and walk up and down until it's dark before making my way back to Katarina's house.

I hesitate as I near the house and almost turn and run but manage to stop myself. I need to get this over with.

I walk up the gravel driveway to the house. The flashy car that I've seen on Katarina's *Instagram* is parked in front of the garage that's attached to the house. It's obviously too much effort to open the garage doors and drive it inside. I almost laugh at the thought of what would happen to that car if it were parked so casually on our estate. In a couple of hours it would either have been stolen or would be minus its wheels and any other removable parts by now. Mac's car only ever escaped being totally trashed because he paid a few of the local layabouts to guard it for him.

The black, painted front door is set back underneath a porch with round arches, and the door is much wider than my own and has an inset of coloured glass in the centre. There is a large brass letterbox flap and doorbell that are polished to an impossible shine. The perfect house for the perfect woman with the perfect life.

The house appears to be in darkness and I guess that Mac is at the back of the house, staying out of sight of any prying neighbours' eyes.

Taking a deep, shuddering breath, I press the doorbell.

CHAPTER SEVENTEEN

The door slowly opens and Mac is standing there in the darkness. He beckons me in, putting his index finger against his lips to tell me to be quiet. I step inside and he closes the front door behind us and walks down the unlit hallway. I follow him through the gloom, just making out the outline of the stairs and several doorways as we pass by.

We go through a doorway and he stops suddenly and I almost walk into him. Instinctively I recoil, not wanting to touch him and I wonder at how I once couldn't get enough of him. He reaches past me and pushes the door shut behind me and then feels along the wall and flicks a switch and the room is flooded with light.

I blink several times, the sudden bright light a shock to my senses. When my eyes have adjusted to the light, I see that we're in an enormous kitchen with a huge island down one end and a vast dining table and chairs at the other. A bottle of champagne and two glasses are placed neatly in the middle of the island, a fancy corkscrew next to them. As I look around, I recognise parts of this kitchen from *Instagram* but the photographs don't do justice to the size of it.

Mac looks at me and grins.

'Quite a place, huh?'

'It is,' I agree, walking to the island and gazing around.

'No one can see us,' he says, nodding at the huge drapes running the length of the end of the kitchen. 'Didn't even have to pull them shut, just press a button and away they go.'

I walk over to the drapes and pull the edge of one curtain aside and peer outside into the darkness of the garden. The neighbours will have no idea that there's anyone inside this house.

'Don't let any light out,' Mac says. 'Don't want any nosey sods poking their noses in.'

I slip off my cagoule and lay it over one of the kitchen chairs and look at Mac who hasn't moved since we came into the room. He's made no move to touch me, nor I him, and I realise how unusual this is.

'So, the plan's all ready, it is, Mac?' I ask, feeling awkward and as if I'm missing something.

'Oh yes, the plan,' Mac says, grinning again.

I stare at him as he turns to look at the kitchen

door and I follow his gaze as the door opens.

'Well, the thing is,' Katarina says, as she steps into the room. 'You're the plan.'

'Have a seat,' Mac says, as if he were a waiter in a restaurant. 'Make yourself comfortable.'

I pull out a high stool from the island and sink onto it, my legs turned to jelly. Mac takes my backpack from my hands and places it on the counter.

'Darling,' Katarina says to Mac. 'Where are your manners, offer Jessica a drink.'

Mac grins his weird smile again and walks over to a wall cupboard and takes out a wine glass and places it next to the two glasses that are already on the counter.

Katarina walks towards me and stands a foot away. She puts her head on one side and studies me and pulls a face.

'I'll agree she looks a little like me Mac, but honestly, the clothes?' She laughs a tinkling laugh and I have a sudden urge to hit her. 'I mean, come on, darling, who actually dresses like that?'

As her eyes sweep over me from head to toe, I study her face. Yes, she looks exactly like me but there's a petulance to her expression and a slight sneer to her lips; a spoiled brat, as Mum would say. She soon tires of looking at me and turns away and I stand up from the stool and reach towards my bag but Mac pulls it smartly out of my reach. He unzips it and puts his hand inside and roots around.

'Mobile phone and a purse, hardly worth the effort of carrying it. Now sit down,' he says, looking at me, the smile now gone. 'And listen.'

I sit back down on shaky legs and Mac walks across to Katarina and gives her my rucksack.

'So,' he says, putting his arm around Katarina and pulling her closer to him. 'We can do this the hard way or the easy way. Either way is fine by me because I'm not averse to a bit of violence, so which is it to be?'

He looks at me as if I'm supposed to know what he's talking about and I stare at him blankly.

'God, you're thick,' he says, rolling his eyes. 'Haven't you caught on yet? I mean, come on, it's not that fucking difficult.'

Katarina giggles and he looks down at her and smiles.

'You've set me up,' I state.

'Well done,' he says. 'Took you a while, though, didn't it?' He smiles again at Katarina who kisses him lightly on the lips and then walks over to the counter and proceeds to start pouring the champagne into the glasses.

'Although I don't understand what I'm being set up for,' I say. 'What's the point of the bank account I opened?'

'Absolutely no point. That was just to keep you involved and make you think we were going to steal something. It was mainly to stop you from getting suspicious. There was a moment when I thought you'd rumbled me. When you questioned why your phone number was on the account? I never thought of that and I'll admit you *almost* impressed me then.'

I stare at him, trying not to blink.

'And then you just carried on and sucked up my lies and I thought, well, you'll be no loss to the world, will you?'

'What do you mean?' I can barely get the words out as my mouth is so dry.

'So,' he says, in a conversational tone. 'What's going to happen is that you're going to have some of this very fine champagne and wash down lots of sleeping tablets that Katarina's been saving up and then you're going to go to sleep and never wake up again.'

My insides turn to water and I think I'm going to be sick.

'But why?' I manage to whisper.

'Because you've just murdered your husband and you can't live with the guilt.' He pulls a mournful face and I hear Katarina giggle again. 'It's all explained in the suicide note that Katarina has written. She's been suffering from depression, you see, hence the sleeping tablets she's been prescribed.' My hands start to shake and I clench them tightly underneath the counter.

They're going to kill me.

Murder.

They've murdered her husband.

'You said you loved me,' I whine, wondering why I'm even bothering to say it.

Mac shrugs and smirks at Katarina.

'It was what you wanted to hear. And I made you happy in your shitty little life for a while, so there is that.'

'I'm sorry, my poor little lookalike,' Katarina says, not sounding sorry at all. 'But I'm the only woman he's ever loved. You were just *useful*.'

'You know he's been sleeping with me?' I say to Katarina. 'We had sex every night and he wasn't faking that so how can you even trust him? He couldn't keep his hands off me.'

She laughs.

'Well, he's a man, darling, he's hardly going to refuse if it's offered on a plate, is he? And the way I heard it, you couldn't keep your hands off him. I'm afraid that it was just lust and nothing more.'

He's discussed me with her and despite not wanting to, I start to cry and don't even try to stop, because what would be the point?

How could I have been so stupid?

Mac sighs.

'Look, if it makes you feel any better, it's nothing personal, you just happen to look like Katarina and we couldn't waste an opportunity like that. Katarina will take your name so in a strange sort of way you'll live on.'

I put my head down and continue to sob whilst slipping my hand underneath my sweatshirt. I work my fingers inside the body tape that is holding the syringe in place and it gradually comes free. I slip the syringe inside the sleeve of my sweatshirt so that it's out of sight. I have no idea what I'm going to do but I'm not giving up without a fight.

'Come on,' Mac says, with an edge to his voice. 'It's no use crying because that's not going to change anything.'

'What if I refuse to swallow the sleeping tablets?' I ask, sniffing.

'Then I'd have to make you, and it won't be pretty. Ask Jonathan, Katarina's husband.' He grins and laughs. 'Oh, no, wait, no you can't, because he's dead.'

I stare at the pair of them and try to get a grip on my fear and think of a way out of this. I have only one syringe even though there is enough GHB in there to knock out an elephant. I told Seamus that I was having a party and needed two bottles of it, but he was reluctant to give it to me. The money persuaded him, as did the threat of what Mac would do to him if he told Mum. But Mac and Katarina are hardly going to stand still for me while I inject them with it, are they? Maybe if I can knock Mac out, I can overpower Katarina and make a run for it.

The sound of the doorbell pierces the silence and Mac looks at Katarina in alarm.

'You're not expecting anyone, are you?' he asks.

'Of course, not, silly, everyone thinks we're away on holiday.'

'Go and have a look,' he says, frowning. 'But don't put the lights on, look out of the lounge window and see if you recognise them.'

'Let's just ignore it,' she says.

'No.' Mac shakes his head. 'Go and look just in case it's one of your nosey neighbours and they heard something. We don't want anyone getting the idea that there's been a break in and calling the police.'

'Oh, okay.' Katarina sighs, as she chucks my rucksack onto the dining table.

The doorbell shrills again and Mac walks over to the light switch and dims the lights and then opens the kitchen door and Katarina slips out into the hallway. Mac stands behind the kitchen door with it slightly open and watches her.

'Don't even think about screaming,' he says to me, quietly. 'Unless you want whoever's at that front door to die with you.'

It's now or never.

I slip the syringe down my sleeve and into my hand and carefully pull the cap off the end. I stretch my arm over to the glasses and press the plunger and inject some of the liquid into the farthest one.

'What are you doing?' Mac snarls.

'Getting a drink,' I say, in a timid voice.

He glances over at me in the gloom and I drag the nearest glass along the counter and put it in front of me. When he turns back to the doorway, I quickly squirt the rest of the syringe into the other glass and return my hand to my lap. I pray that the GHB has gone into the glasses and not all over the counter top.

I take a deep breath and try to calm myself. I need to hide the syringe because if they find it, they'll know what I've done.

They may not even drink the champagne.

Perhaps I should just drink it myself and sink into oblivion.

I push the thought away and with shaking fingers I carefully replace the cap on the needle of the syringe and push it into my jeans pocket.

'Jehovah's Witnesses,' Katarina says, squeezing through the door and coming back into the kitchen. 'A man and a woman. I've seen them before; they're always knocking on doors around here looking for converts.'

'Fuck's sake,' Mac says, closing the kitchen door and turning the lights back up. 'Why do they waste their time?'

Katarina shrugs.

She walks over to me and sits on the opposite side of the counter and reaches out a hand to pick up a glass of champagne. I try to keep my face impassive while she takes several sips. Mac stands at the end of the counter and picks his glass up.

I hold my breath.

'Cheers,' he taunts, holding his glass up in the air at me.

I pick my glass up and take a sip so that my face doesn't betray me.

'Can't beat a glass of Bolly,' he says, as he tips his head back and swallows the glassful in one go.

He puts the glass down on the counter and then picks up the bottle and refills his glass. He looks at Katarina with a questioning look.

'Oh, go on then,' she giggles. She swallows down the champagne and he refills her glass. He puts the bottle down and they gaze at each other as if I'm not even here.

I pretend to sip my champagne and wonder how long it will take.

And as it turns out, not very long at all.

CHAPTER EIGHTEEN

'Christ, I feel a bit pissed,' Mac says, slurring his words.

Katarina looks at him vacantly and wobbles on the stool before grabbing the counter to steady herself.

'Oh, dear,' I say, quietly.

Mac looks at me as he lurches sideways and nearly falls over. He grabs hold of the counter and hauls himself upright.

'What have you done?' he asks, the words slurred and unformed.

'Drugged you,' I say. 'But don't worry, you'll be fine in the morning.'

He looks at me in disbelief, his mouth hanging open slackly and I can't help smiling.

There's a crash as Katarina topples from her stool onto the floor and I wince as I hear her hit the tiles. Hopefully she's broken a bone or two. Mac stares down at her, his mouth hanging open, eyes glazed.

'You underestimated me, Mac,' I state.

'Wha....?'

'I have trust issues, Mac, I did tell you. And as everyone knows, trust issues make a person suspicious.'

I don't know if he even hears me as he slides onto the floor next to Katarina, but it matters not.

I jump down from the stool and walk round to where they're laying; I take hold of Katarina's arm and knee and pull her on her side into the recovery position that I learned on the first aid course that I attended when I was at school. It was a long time ago but I'm quite pleased with my attempt, it was much easier than I thought it would be and Katarina's airway is now protected and she's unlikely to choke should she vomit. I repeat the process with Mac, which takes a bit more effort as he's a lot bigger, but after a bit of huffing and puffing I manage to achieve it.

I don't know how long they'll be out for; it wasn't really a question that I could ask Seamus. Hopefully, I didn't give them so much that it'll kill them because I want them to pay for what they've done. They've had a lot of GHB so I'm hoping it'll be hours before they wake up but I don't intend being here for very long. As soon as I have what I need I'll be gone.

Just in case they should wake up, I take the

largest knife out of the knife block on the counter and take it with me. I don't know if I'm even capable of using it but I feel better for holding it.

I cross the kitchen and pick up my rucksack and then put my cagoule on and go out into the hallway. Using the torch on my phone I check the lounge; another massive room that my entire flat would fit into easily, but that's not what interests me. There's a suitcase and a handbag in the middle of the lounge and I head towards it. I loop the handbag around my neck and drag the case behind me out into the hallway and then along into the kitchen, closing the door behind me.

I check on Mac and Katarina; they're both breathing deeply and haven't moved from their positions. I un-loop the handbag from my neck and open it and look inside to see two passports. I take them out and open them; the first one is Mac's and the second one is mine. There's nothing else of interest in the handbag except for Katarina's purse but I leave it in there and put my passport in my bag and return Mac's to Katarina's handbag. I put the handbag on one of the dining table chairs and then lay the case down on the floor and pray that it's not locked.

It's not; I open it and lay the lid down. It's neatly packed with clothes; mostly Katarina's but some of Mac's that I recognise. In the centre of the suitcase there's a shoe box and I unclip the straps that stretch across it and take it out.

I take the lid off and look inside.

It's full of money.

Bundles and bundles of fifty-pound notes in plastic bands packed tightly together.

So much money.

I have no intention of counting it now so I take out one of the bundles and slip it into my rucksack. I replace the box in the middle of the case, do the straps up and close the case and stand it upright.

I'll be taking that with me.

But first I have to go upstairs.

I dim the kitchen lights and go out into the hallway with my torch and make my way upstairs. The landing is so large that it even has a sofa on it. How can Katarina have all this and still not be satisfied?

There are five doors leading off the landing and they're all closed except for one. I take a deep breath and head for the open doorway.

I stand in the doorway of the bedroom and will myself not to vomit, I swallow down the bile in my throat and remind myself that throwing up all over the floor will not help. When I scanned my torch around the room, I couldn't miss the body lying across the bed nor the large knife handle sticking upright out of its chest. Her husband. What a heartless bitch.

I steel myself and point the beam of the torch onto the body's head; if there's any chance that he's still alive, I have to help him. One look tells me that he's dead; his face is grey, his features frozen into a grotesque scream. I wonder how long he's been dead. I swing the beam of the torch at the floor; there's blood all around the bed, on the carpet and the quilt that I've seen so many times in Katarina's posts on *Instagram* is soaked red. I can't go into the room because if I tread in the blood my footprints will be all over the carpet. I back out of the door and try to imagine where they were intending on leaving me to die; it can't be in here; it must be another room.

I walk along the landing and tighten my grip on the knife. I should just leave now, my brain screams at me, while I still can.

I ignore what the sensible part of me is saying and open the next door and scan my torch around, the room is empty save for an exercise bike and a treadmill. I close the door and continue down the landing.

The next room has a double bed and a huge dresser in it and there on the bed is a sheet of paper. I cross quickly to the bed and pick it up and shine the torch on it.

To whom it may concern... it begins. It's the suicide note and this room was where I was going to spend my dying moments. I pull my rucksack off my shoulder and stuff the letter inside and zip it up.

I run back down the stairs and go into the kitchen, holding the knife out in front of me as I open the kitchen door. I needn't have bothered; Mac and Katarina are still unconscious on the floor. I take the knife to the sink and carefully wipe it with a piece of the luxury paper towel that hangs on a roll beneath the cupboard. I place the knife back into the knife block. I pick up my glass of champagne from the counter top and tip the contents down the sink and then rinse the glass and dry it with the paper towel. I replace the glass in the cupboard where I saw Mac take it from.

I walk over to Mac and slowly push the toe of my boot into his throat. He makes a funny choking sound but otherwise doesn't move. I take my foot away, resisting the urge to kick him repeatedly in the face and mar his handsome good looks. I'm not a violent person but for what they were going to do to me, and what they've done to Katarina's husband, my revenge is restrained.

Although it will be sweet.

I take my rucksack off my shoulder and put it on properly across my back with my arms through the straps so that I have full use of my limbs. I walk over to the suitcase and pull it upright and pick it up and test the weight of it. It's heavy but I'll be able to carry it until I get to the end of the street when I can put it down and tow it. I don't want any of the neighbours to hear me dragging it across the gravel driveway. I pull out the handle and drag it down the hallway and stand it by the front door and come back into the kitchen.

I walk over to the noticeboard and study the wall-mounted telephone next to it. It's sleek and black and, no doubt, very expensive. No one I know has a landline, we use our mobile phones for everything so why bother?

Using the paper towel that I dried the knife and glass with, I pick up the handset, being careful not to let my fingers touch it. I don't think the police will be checking for fingerprints but why take the chance. I press the buttons; 999.

When the operator answers I ask for the police and I'm put through immediately.

'You need to come now', I say, slowly, Katarina style, talking over the call handler. 'I've killed my husband.' I replace the handset and stuff the paper towel up my sleeve.

That's it.

I'm all done here.

CHAPTER NINETEEN

Eight Months' Later

I've discovered that I have quite an aptitude for languages, well, Spanish anyway. I've joined a class and go twice a week to practise and I'm not boasting when I say that I'm the best student there even though I've been attending for the shortest time.

There's an app for Spanish, of course, and I practise every day because I really enjoy it and I want to speak it well. And I have a job too, in a bar, so I get to practise it even more when the Spanish customers come in. I'm even picking up a bit of German as well, so who knows what I could have done if I've gone to a half-decent school.

Not that it matters now; I'm quite content with my life and I have prospects, as they say. Although it has been a little bit tricky staying in Europe for so long, what with Brexit and the whole *no staying more than ninety-days-out-of-a-hundred-and-eighty* thing. But, as with most things, if you have money then all problems are eventually solvable.

And I have money.

A lot of money.

Not that anyone would realise that I have lots of money because I'm not splashing it around. I'm only spending it on what I need and living sensibly because I want it to last, and also, I don't want to draw attention to myself by behaving like a lottery winner. But I do have nice clothes now; not designer, but good quality stuff from good shops, not knock offs from the market or *Primark*.

I'm enjoying working, because waitressing in a Spanish bar in the sunshine hardly seems like working at all. Serving customers who are happy because they're on holiday beats working in a shop or being a cleaner in dreary old England. The customers chat to me as if I'm a friend, they don't treat me like a skivvy who's not worth talking to like they do back in the UK. I've made a few friends too, so I'm not lonely, I always have someone to pal up with for a night out or a shopping trip.

And it's so cheap to live here, too. I have a gorgeous little apartment within walking distance of the beach, it has a balcony and only costs half what that horrible old flat used to cost me. It has decent furniture and a shower that works properly and it's so cheap to eat out that I hardly ever cook.

Realistically, it's going to take a long time for me to make all that cash from the shoe box spendable, because it's a lengthy process laundering money, but I'm getting there. That's the good thing about living in Spain, if you go into a bureau de change and change pounds into Euros, no one bats an eyelid because they assume that you're a tourist. But I do have to do it slowly and spread it around different places so that I don't attract attention.

But I don't mind because I have all the time in the world; I have the rest of my life.

Unlike Katarina and Mac.

I take a sip of my water and tap the newspaper app on my phone. That's the beauty of the internet; I may be sitting here in the blazing sunshine taking my afternoon break but I can still keep up to date on everything that's going on back home.

Today's headlines are all about the trial for the murder of Jonathan Hepworth-Jones. After two days a majority verdict has been reached and Mac and Katarina will be going away for a very long time, as I knew they would be. They were caught practically red-handed and even though no fingerprints were found on the handle of the knife that killed her husband, the facts were plain to see. Even though Katarina had the very best of lawyers, the evidence was too strong – even though she did try and blame Mac for everything. She protested that Mac killed her husband and not she, but the fact that they have her on tape admitting the murder when she telephoned the police says otherwise. Mac, in turn, blamed her. That, more than anything, made my day when I heard it, the fact that they turned on each other to save their own skins.

The money taken from Jonathan Hepworth-Jones' bank accounts and investments has never been recovered but the jury were never in any doubt that greed was the motive behind his murder.

I would say they'll be going away for life but life doesn't mean actually mean life now, does it? But hopefully they'll have an unpleasant time of it in prison and they'll no longer be young when they get out.

Although at least they'll be alive, unlike poor Jonathan.

'Anything interesting, Jess?'

I look up to see Ray, the owner of the bar, standing in front of me.

I hold my phone up to show him the headline.

'A right nasty pair,' I say. 'Got what they deserved.'

'Yeah,' he says. 'Been reading about them, hope they go down for a very long time.

'Me too.' I turn my phone away from him and start to read, hoping he'll take the hint and leave me alone. This is my break and I don't want to waste it talking to him.

He hovers for a moment and then moves to the next table and picks up the empty glasses and takes them to the bar. I flick through the rest of the news and then put my mobile down and turn my face to the sun.

It's so perfect here, I just love it.

Ray, unfortunately, is not so perfect. He's the wrong side of forty although he pretends to be thirty-five and he's made no secret of the fact that he's got the hots for me. I've been keeping him at arms' length but he's persistent and seems to think that he's God's gift to women.

He's nosey, too.

I may have to get a job elsewhere, which won't be a problem because there's always work for an English girl who can speak the language. It'd be a shame, though, because I like it here and I like Ray, too, I just don't want to be his girlfriend.

Because like I've said before.

I've got trust issues.

THE END

Thank you so much for reading this book, I really do appreciate it. I do hope that you've enjoyed it and if you have, I'd be thrilled if you took the time to leave a review or star rating on Amazon/and or Goodreads.

Printed in Dunstable, United Kingdom

84616686R00107